The Long Night of the Grave

CHARLES L. GRANT

Cover art by Jill Bauman

First Crossroad Press Edition

For Don Grant, the godfather of this trilogy; With great affection, with great respect, with the only way I know to rightfully thank him; and wishing I could claim him a blood relation as well.

Chapter 1

Spring, the dying season; when the comfort of the day's warmth is sapped by blind stars, and the blind deadgrey moon sets a chill in the air that makes bootheels sound brittle and voices sound thin, that kills new blossoms with a wind's winter razor and new growth marks time until its browning in autumn; when sleep after midnight fills with unsettled dreams because the season is unsettled and unsettles the minds of those who know that the year always returns to the color of the dead.

Spring, the dying season; when a thick rolling mist rises from the creek circling the base of Pointer Hill, and drifts from the wetlands on the north side of the valley, seeping from the rotting wood at the bottom of deadfalls, the nightside of boulders, moving without a breeze to caress greying bark, to cover scattered gnawed bones, to ride toward the moon and fall back again, twisting into a striped and shifting cloud that too often resembles smoke from the ashes of a damp fire.

Spring, whose afternoons are the time for walking, dusk the time for heading home.

And night the time for listening for someone moving behind you.

Silently.

Slowly.

With the stealth of a formless shadow.

But Thorny knew it was only the twinges of his weary legs and the stir of his imagination. There was no one on the road with him, and there hadn't been since midafternoon when a tinker rolled by on a cart so loaded with junk, the passing sounded like an army using tin sticks for swords. He wasn't surprised. From what his colleagues over to Harley had told him around the fire burning low beside the railroad tracks, there wasn't much traffic between the rest of Connecticut and the village he sought. Which made it just fine as far as he was concerned. No one to see him, therefore no one to place him.

He smiled, spat, wiped his salt-and-pepper beard with a grimy sleeve, and sniffed.

A loud sigh for company.

A roll of his shoulders to ease the weight of his bedroll.

A kick of his leg sideways to ease the stiffness in the thigh, and a slow and deep breath to take in the air newly touched with young leaves.

A great night for walking—the moon big as God's eye, enough of a breeze to keep the goddamn bugs from his ears, and the temperature just cool enough to keep the sweat from gathering under his coarse shirt.

And that, he promised himself, would be the first thing he'd take care of once he'd taken care of the first house. A new shirt from the finest shop, one of them silk things with the pleats and ruffles down the front made just for him, and maybe one of them vicuna morning suit things with the long cutaway jackets, the fancy waistcoats with shiny pearl buttons, and grey striped trousers with creases so sharp he could cut a throat just by kicking.

He'd seen hundreds of them clothes, maybe even thousands of them, out in Chicago at the Columbian Exposition. Everybody wearing them like everybody was rich. The electric lights. The hoochy-cooch dancers. Jesus God, it had been like falling into heaven with both eyes open. Of course he hadn't been able to stay long, what with the blues spotting him right

The Long Night of the Grave

away and chasing him halfway to creation and back again before he hopped the train; but that didn't matter. Soon as he got them clothes, he was going back, and he was going to parade in front of them snot-nosed cops and dare them to do something about it.

His stride lengthened.

A tune whistled in the moonlight.

And then he came to the top of the curving rise and looked down the long road.

There were soft lights, warm lights off near the horizon, beyond the hill that rose blackly on his left. On his right there was nothing but trees, and shadows shifting, and nightbirds cawing at him softly, as if telling him it was all right, come in, we won't hurt you.

"Thorny, take it easy," he warned himself then. His imagination working, that's all, nothing more. He wasn't used to moving in the dark like this: he did most of his traveling in daylight, or on trains where the dark didn't matter because it moved too swiftly past him.

He wasn't used to the ground fog that glowed pale under the moon, slipping out of the woods and down off the hill, crossing the road in billowing patches that hid his feet from him and coated his shins with thin ice.

That rose, when the breeze quickened, into a silent white-backed beast hovering on the verge, waiting for him with the nightbirds.

He wasn't used to the quiet that whispered his name.

"Jesus, Thorny," he said, and gave himself a vigorous shudder that put the ground fog in its place and sent the shadows back under the branches and the leaves.

Think of the lights. Those lights, over there. They meant fine houses and fine people. Warm stables for sleep and a drinking hole where he'd learn where all the money was. Only a few minutes away, and only a few hours away from loading the empty spaces of his bedroll with all the gold he could carry. That's what his friends told him: a village like this had all the gold he could carry.

Then he heard the noise, and he knew this time it was real. The distant rattling thunder of a carriage on the move. Behind and below him, lumbering up the hill.

He sniffed again and yanked on the stiff brim of his cloth cap. Stretched his neck, his lips, blinked his eyes and moved over to the verge.

Walking. Always walking. It's what he did best, having done it all the way to the Mississippi and back more times than he could count, dropping in on towns like this, dropping out a few nights later on the wheels of a train.

The thunder grew, the rattling separating into the creaks of springs and the snap of traces and the roll of high wheels over the hard ground.

He frowned.

More than one, he decided after listening a moment. Odd, but nothing to worry about. Just keep walking, keep out of sight, and if they spot you, those so-called friends in Harley were going to pay, and pay dear.

He shifted the bedroll from right shoulder to left and moved closer to the trees when the first carriage came out of the turn, its corner lamps glaring, horses snorting.

He moved into the shadows and watched it pass, a great black brougham with baggage tied atop and behind, its curtains drawn, driver hunched over the reins. Moving steadily but not at a gallop, because, he realized, it probably didn't want to outpace the wagon coming along behind.

Nothing special there either, except it was carrying only a single crate so long and large its end hung over the back and it had to be tied to the vehicle with a webbing of thick rope.

The Long Night of the Grave

Interesting, he thought; someone new moving in.

And he had just stepped back onto the road when the wagon's rear right wheel rolled over a huge rock, slid off, and the bed began to slew to the right. The driver wisely aimed the horses in the same direction so that the forward motion would keep the wagon from tipping.

But it didn't prevent the crate from sliding out from beneath its restraints and crashing to the ground, shattering a cloud of mist and sending the nightbirds flying.

Thorny didn't hesitate. This was a chance to do a good deed and meet a possible benefactor, and such chances were too few and far between not to explore.

He ran toward the crate, shouting as he did to warn the driver he'd lost his cargo.

The brougham slowed, finally stopped, the wagon pulling up alongside it.

Thorny reached the crate first and dropped the bedroll at his feet. Shaking his head. Tsking. Scrubbing his hands as though nervous about the operation before him. The crate had split open, several planks from its long side pulled from their nails and lying on the road.

"Not to worry, sir," he said with his best smile when he saw the driver heading toward him. "You're in luck, and that's the truth. Thornton Narbuck at your service, the best damned carpenter in the whole damned state. Give me a good flat rock and a few minutes, and I'll have your baggage back together good as new."

He spit on his hands to prove his good intentions and squinted at the ground, kicking at the mist until he found what he wanted. He reached down for the rock, and felt a hand on his shoulder.

"No need," he said cheerfully. "I can manage, sir, thank you."

The grip tightened, and straightened him, and before he could react his back was bent the other way and something cold, smooth, and sharp was drawn across his wattled throat.

Salt in his mouth and dampness flooding over his chest, and when he felt his knees weaken, the hand released him, and he fell.

Feeling nothing when he landed on his face and no one to catch him.

Seeing nothing but the moonlight, and the mist crawling toward him.

Hearing nothing but his own gagging, and the frantic pounding of his heart.

Watching the moonlight fade, watching the crate being dragged away, and seeing through the ragged gap what had to be a coffin. A huge coffin of a type he had never seen in his life.

And a face on the side, large blue eyes, large red mouth, silver and gold all around, all the gold he could carry if he could only move his hands, if only he could stop screaming and no one now to hear him.

———

Spring: the dying season; and the carriage moved on slowly, the wagon moving on behind it, past the hill on the left and the deserted farmland on the right, until it came to a road the ground fog left alone and the moonlight paved with silver. And when it turned the lamps went out, the wheels rolled softly, and for a moment spring was winter in the village of Oxrun Station.

Chapter 2

The new police station on Chancellor Avenue was less than three years old, but already those who worked there spoke of it as if it had been there forever. They complained of the cold in winter, the heat in summer, the feeling that every time they approached its Roman temple façade they ought to throw on togas and crash through the high double doors demanding the heads of Christians.

John Vicar knew how they felt. It looked stupid. It didn't belong. But the architect had been brother to a village council's leader, and stupid or not, the marble and the pillars were to some awfully impressive. Thank god, he thought as he approached the wooden railing at the back of the waiting room, that Lucas Stockton hadn't lived to see it. He would have resigned as Chief on the spot and moved to the highest mountain in Maine.

The sergeant on duty was behind a long wood desk set on a platform half a foot above the floor. When he saw John at the railing gate he put down a pen and eyed him warily, and John grinned his most innocent.

"You know," a laughing Ned Stockton had told him once, "one of these days you're going to learn to control that mind of yours, and when you do, all those wonderful ideas are going to vanish."

That had been said the evening he and Ned had sat in the Brass Ring on Steuben Avenue, drinking ale and pondering what had seemed to be an unsolvable murder. John had had a sudden notion, blurted it out, and two days later saw Ned and Tom Alden haul in the killer.

Since that time he had taken unwilling part in a handful of puzzling cases that had been—accidentally, he was sure—solved through his efforts.

"Afternoon, Mr. Vicar."

"And a good afternoon to you, Sgt. Alden."

"The chief's away," the burly man growled.

"I know. Gallivanting blithely with wife and family across Europe while you're forced to stay here and deal with dolts like me when you have more important things to do."

Alden's perpetually flushed face didn't alter its expression, and John sighed. Though the others on the force tolerated his dropping in now and then with at least a semblance of good humor, this one plain and simply didn't like him. The feeling was mutual, but John wasn't going to show it.

"Actually," he said, taking off his boater and holding it to his chest, "I was hoping to catch Cab in. Is he around?"

"Out."

"Ah."

"Don't know when he'll be back."

"I see."

"Been gone since morning."

"Oh. Too bad."

Alden pointedly looked down at a stack of papers on his desk and picked up the pen, licked the nib and dipped it into an inkwell. Then he looked up without raising his head, the message clear enough.

"Well, then, Sergeant," John said with another smile, "I'll be moving on then. Would you please tell Detective Planter I was asking for him?"

The Long Night of the Grave

No response but a stare, and he left before he decided to take off the man's head. Stood on the top step and blindly watched the traffic on the broad sunlit avenue. He had been hoping to find out if Cab had learned anything about the body discovered by a farmer on Mainland Road the morning before. A slit throat and a bedroll with several gold coins hidden in its folds had ruled out, it seemed to him, an accident and highway thievery. But no one seemed to care much; the man was unknown and unknown he would probably remain.

But John hated loose ends like he hated the silly costumes women wore these days when they played at playing lawn tennis in the park, dancing about and squealing so that the young men who watched them would grow warmer than the weather.

Just the way he did himself, especially when the woman was Betty Jerrard, who never played at anything unless she played to win.

Ah well, he thought with benign resignation as he placed the straw hat on his head and slapped at a lock of sandy hair that sprang out to blind one eye; even if Cab had learned something, the detective wouldn't necessarily tell him. Planter was understandably protective of his own slow-growing reputation, and though he hadn't been reluctant to ask John for advice in the past, he wasn't nearly as quick as Ned to fill him in on a case, not until he was stumped.

Besides, he reminded himself with a frown, there were more important things to worry about than what amounted to meddling in something not his affair. Tomorrow, if all went as he feared, he was probably going to incur the righteous wrath of one of his closest friends, and there was nothing he could do about it without ruining the man.

Damn, he thought sadly, and turned up toward Centre Street, pausing briefly at the corner to watch an elegant carriage rumble past. A glimpse of a woman inside, and a man beside her. A glimpse, nothing more, of features that on Westerners might seem rather coarse, but on them were perfect, exotic, and on the woman altogether lovely.

When they were gone, he crossed over and hurried up to High Street, turned right and walked quickly past the abandoned Bartlett's Livery, smiling fondly at the decrepit structure and envisioning it the way it should be, the way it would be before the summer was over.

And the way he prayed it would be in years ahead, or what was left of his father's money would vanish as if it were nothing but air.

A horn blared at him, and he jumped backward, not realizing he had stepped off the curb until a polished black electric had nearly run him down. He tipped his hat at the woman driving and at the ladies upright and prim in the back seat, and watched them as they putted up to the Pike and vanished around the corner.

His mood lightened.

He laughed quickly and shook his head—his future, by god, had almost killed him, and if that wasn't irony then he'd best head back to school.

Another laugh for his dreaming, and he rushed across the street and into the park where he spent the rest of the afternoon watching the ladies play lawn tennis as he cursed their silly costumes, cursed the young men hanging around them and calling out encouragement at every fine play and at every mistake.

Betty Jerrard wasn't there.

And by the time his stomach protested his lack of eating, the sun was already low, a chill in the air, the leaves whispering overhead as a north wind swept down out of the darkening sky. He rose with a groan, scolding himself for wasting time like that, for dozing, for daydreaming, and for thinking that Betty would somehow read his mind and flee her sister's home just to join him.

A dusting off of his trousers, and he left the park, walked up to the Pike, and turned right. Moving steadily, with long strides, habit long since telling him when to slow down, when to pick up his feet and get a move on. If all went well, he'd arrive home just in time for dinner and be spared Mrs. Karragan's poor imitation of a mother hen; if all went well, the meal wouldn't be burned, or boiled tasteless.

"It's a hard life, Johnny," he told himself with a grin, and only idly glanced left when a brougham drifted by, his attention quickening too late when he realized it carried the man and woman who were staying with Jeffrey Isle.

They had only recently arrived, he'd learned from listening to the gossip in the Chancellor Inn and the Brass Ring. Some said they were from Italy, others said from Egypt. All agreed the man was well-spoken, British educated, and cold as the Atlantic in the middle of winter. On the other hand, the woman traveling with him was reputed to be exotically beautiful, always bedecked in silver, always ready with a smile. Though he hadn't yet met either one, John had seen enough to know that the woman was indeed something to behold, and he only hoped he'd have a chance to check his impressions more closely.

A name came to mind then—Peter Reskin.

He rubbed the back of his neck thoughtfully.

Something else to concern himself about, however unpleasant it was. Reskin was a self-proclaimed archeologist who, despite his rather dubious credentials, had actually been moderately successful in his explorations in the Ottoman Empire and Egypt. Jeffrey was his principal backer. And John had to admit that the man had indeed returned with some impressive artifacts, some of which had been donated to museums in Boston and New York, while others had been sold to those willing to pay the price.

As he himself had been the last time. Last month. When Reskin had appeared at his door late one evening and claimed desperate need of funds. Three pieces had been given over that night—one to John: one to Sydney Edmunds, and one to Howard Turnbell. Unfortunately, and possibly deliberately, Reskin hadn't told Jeffrey Isle what he'd brought back, and Jeffrey was now demanding their return as was, he claimed, his right as the expedition's financier.

His shadow slipped ahead of him, and he watched it mesmerized until a call woke him up and he saw a horseman riding toward him from the direction of the Village. He waited until the man drew abreast, eyeing the sleek black Arabian with suspicion, before starting off again.

"I understand Jeffrey's been after you for money," said Sterling Avlock.

"If he is, I should think it would be our business, not yours," he answered stiffly.

The man laughed and slapped his booted thigh with a riding crop. "Well, my dear Vicar, a word to the wise though you don't deserve it—save your money. The man's not worth it. His trouble doesn't concern you."

And before he could respond, the man was gone, galloping fiercely up the road with coattails flying and crop high in the air. When neither stumble nor branch unseated him, John knew there were no miracles left in the world, and he jammed his hands into his pockets and angled across toward the low wall that fronted his home.

He supposed that Jeffrey Isle had attempted to gain a loan from Avlock as well, and his eyes narrowed slightly. This wasn't right. Though Jeffrey had problems, and serious ones, it wasn't like him to go begging practically door to door. Not only was it out of character, it gave John the immediate feeling that his friend hadn't exactly been honest about the reasons for his need.

He shook himself and scowled. Not now. Think about it later, sleep on it, wait until tomorrow. By then, something might have happened to change the situation, and he wouldn't have to deny the man once again.

He thought then of the missing miracle and sighed aloud.

Sleep, he thought gloomily, wasn't going to come easy.

———

Dark figures in a dark room, and outside the sound of horses impatient in their traces.

An owl watched shadows.

A large brown dog scratched at a door and whimpered, tail between its legs.

"This will not be a good place."

"Don't be silly. No one ever comes here, the door is solid, and I have the only key to the lock."

"It is not good. Wood burns. Wood cracks. A neighbor could pass and see too much and learn."

"In the middle of the night?"

"It matters not when. It could happen. This place is not right. We will have to find another."

"All right, damnit. If you insist."

"I have no choice."

"Then where?"

"Stone. We must have stone. The place I saw this morning."

"My god, you're asking the impossible."

A pause, and the clear sense of a smile.

A laugh, short and mirthless and knowing.

"You're right. What's one more impossibility?"

"There are no impossibilities. There is only that which has not been thought of before, and that which has been forgotten."

"You're a witch, you know."

"No. Just one who has been forgotten."

The rustle of soft cloth, the scrape of a boot, and the grate of a key in a new and easy lock. The door opened and the night relieved the dark of the room.

The owl flew off.

The horses stamped their hooves.

The dog howled and clawed at the other door.

"We will do the moving tomorrow afternoon,"

"What? In broad daylight?"

"Do you not bury your dead while the sun is up?"

"Yes, but—"

"Then so shall we."

"It's crazy. It's—"

"Impossible?"

A footstep on soft ground, and the nightwind rose to multiply the shadows.

"Damn, but I don't know why I'm doing this."

"A lie."

"So it is. But it doesn't make me feel any better."

"Just remember what I have told you, then. Think of how it will be when you do not have to die."

Chapter 3

The small High Street office was well-appointed without ostentation, the furniture large and comfortable, the photographs and prints on the walls wood-framed, the sideboard well stocked with brandy and scotch. The afternoon light was only partially diffused by the closing of the curtains, and through the open window behind them was the sound of children playing hoops in the street, vendors hawking their wares, and the infrequent rude blare of a horn on an impatient electric motor car.

John Vicar, always more than a little uncomfortable in the presence of such unstated wealth and power, stood by the door with his hands clasped behind him and tapped one foot against the floor lightly.

"John," said Sydney Edmunds, "why don't you sit down?"

With a smile he shook his head at the heavyset man in the tailored suit sitting behind a leather-edged mahogany desk.

"I'm all right, Syd."

"Yes, well ..." and Edmunds fussed with some papers on the blotter before him before leaning back in his chair. His fingers tented under his chin; his eyes closed halfway.

"If you don't mind, I'd like to get on with it," Howard Turnbell complained in a voice just short of whining. "I do have a bank to run, you know, and those fools will have me in the gutter if I don't watch them every minute."

Edmunds said nothing.

John only shifted, leaning back so he could cross one foot over the other. A glance up at the high ceiling, and he smiled to himself at the small, crystal chandelier that once held candles and was now electrically wired. He knew Edmunds didn't really trust the invisible power; he hadn't even taken the gas jets from the walls.

"The point," Edmunds began.

"The point, damnit," Jeffrey Isle interrupted, "is that I've been waiting for your answers for days, and all you've done is stall me. That is the point, sir, and I think I have the right to complain, don't you?"

John looked at the young man without turning his head—a dark blue suit tailored to his slender figure, cravat pinned with a ruby, grey gloves on his lap, Wellingtons polished so brightly they reflected the sun. That's all there is to him, he thought suddenly; the ruddy face, the red hair, none of it registers because the man is all clothes and pomp. Naked, he'd be invisible.

He grinned.

"You find the situation humorous, John?" Isle said angrily.

"Now, Jeffrey," Edmunds cautioned.

"Now nothing, Sydney!" The man jabbed a finger in the air, first at Edmunds, then at John. "This has gone on quite long enough, and I have no intention of leaving until you tell me yea or nay."

Turnbell sniffed and glanced pointedly at his pocket watch.

Edmunds folded his fingers down into a double fist and rested his chin upon it. "Jeffrey," he said, in a tone that instantly caught the younger man's attention, "we agreed to meet with you this afternoon because believe it or not we are your friends, and we are concerned for your welfare."

Isle simply stared, his eyes narrowed in anger.

"But," Edmunds continued, "if all you're going to do is make demands, which I ought to remind you are beyond your power to make, then I think we should adjourn. I have business to conduct. And I would guess John does as well."

Isle inhaled deeply, rapidly, several times. "All right, then. Yes. Yes, I apologize. Truly, gentlemen. I have a great deal on my mind these days, and I'm just upset about matters, as I'm sure you can understand."

John and Edmunds immediately nodded their acceptance.

"Wonderful," said Turnbell sourly. "Now that we're all good friends again, I would hope you'll come to the real point and soon."

"I want those pieces, and I want them today," said Isle bluntly.

No one said a word.

No one needed to. Peter Reskin's sale of the Egyptian artifacts to the other men in the room had taken on an importance none of them had foreseen. And once Jeffrey had realized the pieces were missing from the inventory, he wanted them back, and he had no way of paying the prices required.

"Well?" Isle demanded.

Turnbell cleared his throat. "Have you spoken to Mr. Reskin about his part in this, Jeffrey?"

"You know damned well I haven't," he said. "I've been out to his place a dozen times over the past week, and he's not been there. I haven't seen him, have you?"

The banker shook his head.

"Good. Fine. He's probably run off with the money you all gave him. I don't care. All I want is what's rightfully mine. All I want are those pieces back!"

Edmunds looked balefully at the chandelier.

"Oh, for god's sake," Isle snapped. "It's not as if I'm asking you to give them to me outright, is it? I'm good for it. You all know that. You'll have your money soon enough."

John leaned back against the door and scratched the underside of his chin. "Unfortunately, Jeff, soon enough isn't good enough. These are hard times, and they're getting worse. A situation I know you can appreciate. And until someone in Washington makes up his mind which way the standard lies — silver or gold — money isn't worth what it used to be." He smiled blandly. "Isn't that right, Syd? Isn't that what you told me last week?"

Isle snorted angrily and threw himself back in his chair, leaned forward again and appealed to Turnbell with a look. The banker, similarly dressed though minus cravat and ruby, opened a folder on his lap, cleared his throat, reached into an inside jacket pocket and pulled out a pair of glasses. He put them on, adjusted them toward the middle of his nose, and cleared his throat again.

"Oh, for crying out loud," John muttered.

"Jeffrey," the banker said, "you claim you'll be able to pay us within a reasonable amount of time. Unfortunately, you and I both know that's impossible. You are overdrawn, you are in debt, and unless you intend to sell the Hall, you haven't a dream of even giving us what we initially paid."

Isle gaped at him. "What?" he exclaimed angrily. "But for god's sake, man, it's not as if you're exactly starving to death, is it? You've got your bloody bank, Edmunds his railroads ..." He sputtered into silence and lowered his head, shook it slowly. "I need the money," he said in a near whisper. "The men I am in debt to—"

"Common gamblers," the banker sneered.

"—won't wait another week. If I don't pay them, they're going to come after me."

John opened his mouth and shut it again, realizing he had nothing to say; nothing, that is, that would make Jeff feel better.

"I need help," Isle pleaded when the silence grew too long. "Those pieces ... I can turn them over, pay my debts and repay you. Jesus, you won't miss the goddamned money!"

"That isn't the point, Jeffrey," the banker said stiffly.

Isle leapt to his feet, red-faced, knuckles white.

"Easy, Jeff," Edmunds cautioned.

Isle slammed a fist on the desk, his eyes narrowed in rage. "Don't tell me to take it easy, Syd. I haven't the time to take it easy. I ... I." He stopped, drew a breath, closed his eyes. "All right," he said, forcing calm into his voice. "All right. I get it. Good old Jeffrey is a bad risk. Even to his friends. When he's up, that's fine. Slap him on the back, invite him to dinner. But when he's down, kick him like the cur you really think he is."

"Jeff," John protested quietly.

But Isle only glared at him as he gathered up his gloves and walking stick, strode heavily to the rack by the door and yanked down his coat.

John moved away.

Isle grabbed the doorknob and turned. "You're fools, you know," he said tightly. "You don't know what you're doing. You just ... you don't know."

And he was gone before any of them could stop him.

A moment passed before Edmunds rose and sighed loudly.

"The poor fool," Thornbell said with no sympathy at all. "He gambles it away, throws it away on women and extravagance, and yet he expects us to bail him out just like that."

"We have in the past," Edmunds reminded him.

"In the past," the banker said stiffly, "he's come through more often than not. The losses were always recouped later on. But this time he has gone too far. He is asking us to give him those artifacts, hand them over and forget what we gave Reskin, that's what it amounts to. And no matter what he thinks, none of us have that kind of money to throw away."

Reluctantly John agreed, but he couldn't help feeling guilty; nor could he forget the look on Isle's face when he'd stormed out of the office—it wasn't one of rage; the flush had gone from his cheeks, the fury from his eyes, and if John hadn't known the man better, he would have sworn that Isle looked scared to death.

By late afternoon the sky had grown thunderheads like gun powder explosions over a battlefield, and John was ready to scream at the perversities thrown at him from the moment he'd opened his eyes and had seen the first clouds massing over the valley. He had risen late, had been scolded by Mrs. Karragan for making her fix him breakfast so close to the noon hour, had cut himself shaving, and decided that suspenders were God's eighth plague when twice a snap had pulled from its mooring, the metal tip nearly taking out his left eye.

Then there was the meeting at Sydney's office, and the unpleasant feeling that he'd somehow, without knowing it, betrayed a friend.

After walking home in a mood as grey as the clouds above him, he spent the rest of the day outside, huddled in a cardigan and wandering about the grounds, cursing himself for not being able to stop thinking about Jeff.

The man was seven kinds of a fool. The fortune his family had left him was virtually gone now, and his dubious partnership with Peter Reskin had only once in five years produced anything that could conceivably be called profitable.

Yet the man persisted. Driven not only by the need to replenish his coffers, but also to beat what he called the curse of the Isles—none of the males had yet lived past fifty, and Jeffrey was determined to have more than his remaining twenty years.

The Long Night of the Grave

John shook his head with a sigh and leaned against the low stone wall that fronted his land. He himself may not be as wealthy as the men he'd been with today, but if he were careful, and prudent, there was a good chance he might be able to make himself a name. In the meantime there was his home; it wasn't much as estates on the Pike went—a few acres, a modest brick home, a small garden in back he used to bolster his moods whenever he saw his father's ghost in his dreams, or when he thought about his own finances and wondered in fear if his vision of the future wasn't as desperate as his friend's.

A finger rubbed the side of his nose.

Deep in the valley he heard the first muttering of thunder.

Something was wrong.

Jeffrey hadn't told them everything, and John knew it. The two of them had virtually grown up together, there was little the man could hide from him.

Something was wrong.

Jeff had been lying.

Finally he could stand it no longer. He strode around to the back where Mrs. Karragan's husband, Leo, was raking the lawn while whistling an off-key rendition of "Daisy Bell." The man was near sixty, looked ten years younger, and was easily a head taller than the man who employed him. With his shirtsleeves rolled up, he looked like a blacksmith.

"Mr. Karragan," John said.

Karragan raked a few seconds more, then wiped his face with a handkerchief pulled from his hip pocket. "Sir?"

"Would you like a break?"

The man's deeply tanned face wrinkled in a smile. "Wouldn't say no, sir."

"I want to get a message to Mr. Isle. Would you mind?"

Karragan looked toward the house where his wife was watching him closely from the kitchen window. "Not at all. If you'll give me a moment to clean up a bit … ?"

John smiled, blew a kiss toward the kitchen, and walked to the front wall again, just as a pair of electrics thumped by over the rutted road. Rains the week before, followed by unusually warm weather, had made the Pike miserable to travel on, another reason why he preferred walking, though it was more than a mile into the village. His neighbors, when they bothered talking to him at all, thought him odd not to have a full stable or a garage, and when he suggested that walking was good for the body and soul, they reminded him that walking in the rain was just as apt to kill him as falling from a saddle.

He turned around and rested his elbows on the walls, staring blindly at the house while waiting for Karragan.

Jeffrey Isle.

He frowned.

And was still frowning when a hand reached over the wall and grabbed his shoulder.

Chapter 4

"Jesus!" John yelled, and whirled about so violently that his feet became tangled and he fell to the grass.

A woman laughed gaily.

He looked up at the face peering over the fieldstone and decided that the only sensible thing to do now was crawl back into bed and hide his head until tomorrow.

"Good afternoon," he said glumly.

Betty Jerrard winked at him, her face clear and round beneath a pale green cap that fit so snugly it fluffed out the sides of her short brown hair. When he stood, slowly, he could see she was wearing her cycling costume-puffed sleeves on a green overblouse open to the waist and revealing the white silk blouse beneath; her legs were covered with bloomer-like pants, and when she posed prettily beside her bicycle, he couldn't help grinning .

"You're a picture, and that's a fact," he said, resting his forearms on the wall.

"You think it's silly," she replied, glancing down at her outfit. "You think it makes me look like I've swallowed a balloon."

He laughed. It did. And when she laughed in return, he could not help but stare at the large brown eyes, the full lips, the color in her cheeks. Too many of his dreams were taken by her presence, yet too many of his waking hours reminded him that her brother-in-law, Sterling Avlock, had little use for the Vicars, and less use for the sole survivor.

"Do you want to come?" she said, nodding east toward the valley. "I'm going out to see the colts."

"I don't think so," he answered with genuine regret. "I've things to do, I'm afraid."

Her face clouded.

"Really," he insisted gently. "I do."

"Well," she said brightly, "the least you can do for the insult is have dinner with me Friday evening."

He would have laughed had he not seen the look on her face. "You're serious."

"Of course I am, silly. Sterling is not a complete ogre, you know."

Somewhat flustered, he was about to render his regrets when Karragan came up behind him, dressed in brown-and-gold livery that had seen better days. John had given up trying to tell the man that such dress was inappropriate, at least for him, but the Karragans had been with the family too long to change.

With an apologetic glance at Betty, he asked Leo to see if Mr. Isle wouldn't please join his friend for dinner this evening. A matter of some importance. Karragan's face made no secret of his distaste for the Isles, and young Jeffrey, but he nodded and swung himself astride a bicycle he'd wheeled from the almost empty stables on the right side of the house. The vehicle was too small for the size of the man; Karragan's knees were at comical angles from the front wheel, and Betty giggled as soon as the man was out of earshot.

"For heaven's sake, John," she said, "the man is ancient. Why don't you let him ride?"

"He doesn't much like horses," he said, his gentle mood gone as he watched the old man's back. In truth, the only animals left in the stable were a roan he rode for distances longer than he felt like walking, and a sullen old mare used only for the carriage. Karragan hated her and refused to use her more than he had to; the roan was John's, and no one could ride it but him.

"And speaking of horses, didn't you purchase the Bartlett Livery?"

He looked at her sharply, and instantly regretted it when she stared at the ground in guilt.

"Sorry," she said. "I guess I'm not to know that, am I."

He wanted to be angry, to demand how she'd found out, but when her woebegone expression wasn't able to hold and soon broke into an impish grin, he grinned himself and sighed loudly.

"I have no secrets from you, do I?" he said.

"Then you have?"

He nodded. "I'm going to rebuild it as soon as I can, if you must know it all. Clear it all out, get rid of the stalls and, with a bit of luck, the smells too. Then I'm going to sell motor cars."

Her mouth opened, but nothing came out.

"Terrible, isn't it," he said in mock sadness. "What a thing for the Vicars to come to, selling merchandise like an ordinary shopkeeper."

"But John, that's wonderful!" she exclaimed. "My god, you're going to make a fortune!"

He held up one hand and crossed his fingers, though he was unable to hide his pleasure that at last someone didn't think he was a complete fool all the time.

"When are you going to start?" she asked excitedly.

"As soon as I can. By summer's end, with luck."

The sound of a carriage approaching from the east made him glance over, then back.

Betty looked as well, shrugged, and said, "And is Jeffrey going to be your partner?"

"Ah. He's spoken to you then."

She nodded. "Just this morning, as a matter of fact. He came to see Sterling and barely had a dozen words for me. He was terribly upset."

John wondered what she'd say if she'd seen him after the meeting at Syd Edmunds'. Then, without thinking, he told her about Isle's gambling debts and his desperate attempts to regain possession of Reskin' s sales. And as he spoke, he wondered aloud if perhaps the items had in fact been stolen.

"Reskin wouldn't be above that sort of thing," he said.

Her eyes widened in fascination. "Really? But I thought he was a professor or something."

"He calls himself that, true. But as far as Sydney or I can determine, the man has no credentials save those of an interested amateur."

Excitement brought a deeper glow to her face, and she bit lightly on her lower lip. "Yet he's successful, isn't he? I mean, Sterling is always saying that Mr. Reskin has delivered more important finds to museums than anyone else except the British."

"I wouldn't know about that," he said. And he slapped a palm against his thigh. "Damn, why didn't I think of it before? Lord, Jeff could be covering up for problems with the authorities. Not only here but in Egypt as well. Damn!"

Betty raised a finger. "John," she cautioned.

He knew without her saying it—his own curse of leaping to conclusions had more than once dropped him into hot water, and more than once during their lives had Betty and Jeff saved him from his own too-quick tongue.

The difference now was—Betty hadn't changed, and Jeffrey certainly had.

The Long Night of the Grave

"Anyway, that's why I need to see him," he said, indicating with a nod the direction Karragan had taken. "I don't like it when we fight. It serves no purpose except to get us both upset. And I need to talk some sense into him, Betty. If he goes on like this, he's going to end up in jail. Or worse. And I can't help the feeling that he's not telling me everything he should. He acts as if …" He waved a hand in frustration. "Damn, I don't know. I just wish I knew what to do."

She started to say something, but never had the chance. The carriage, a sleek black brougham, swept up the Pike at a rate that made its gilt-edged wheels roll over the earth like thunder. The driver was hunched over on his high perch, furiously whipping the air above matched bays whose heads were high and whose flanks were touched with flecks of lather. He was about to comment on its speed when, just before it drew abreast of them, the near front wheel dropped into a deep rut.

With a harsh squeal of springs and wood the vehicle heeled sharply to the left, and the driver shouted his anger at the animals who were pulling frantically the other way. Immediately, John cried out a warning as he vaulted the wall, grabbing Betty and spinning her away from the looming carriage, just before the wheel popped out of the rut again and its back end slewed around within inches of where she'd been standing.

The whip cracked.

One of the bays whickered and snorted.

And the carriage moved on without slowing down.

"Damned idiot," he said. "Christ, he could have killed you."

"An accident," she said weakly. "I'm …"

When she swayed he slipped a quick arm around her waist and, when she did not protest, moved her gently to the wall so she could lean against it.

"Are you all right?" he asked, concerned for the lack of color in her cheeks and the way her arms trembled as she hugged herself tightly.

"I think so."

"He's an idiot," he muttered again.

And they watched in silence as the speeding brougham swerved alarmingly to the right several hundred yards up the road and vanished up a drive.

It was heading for Isle Hall.

John jammed his hands into his pockets and glared as if he could bring the driver back for an apology. "It's that guest of Jeffrey's," he said, walking toward the center of the road and back again. "I don't know his name. Far as I know, Jeff hasn't invited anyone over to even meet him." And he stopped when he saw the look on Betty's face. "You know him?"

She nodded, her color slowly returning, her breathing growing more calm. "His name is Khirhal Bey," she answered quietly. "He has something to do with Jeffrey's partner."

"Reskin?" he said, astonished. "Peter Reskin?"

"Yes. At least I think so. Sterling says Mr. Bey and his wife are something like aristocrats in their country. I gather they're quite wealthy."

"You don't say."

Betty came to stand beside him. "Do you think he has something to do with Jeff's trouble?"

He managed a brief smile. "I doubt even Jeff could get in gambling trouble that far from home without leaving home himself. I would guess, though, that your Mr. Bey might have something to do with those things Jeffrey wants to buy back."

A glance at Betty who was swinging aboard her bicycle, and he looked back at the place where the carriage had swept out of sight.

"About dinner Friday," he began.

The Long Night of the Grave

"Eight o'clock," she said. And as she passed him, a coy glance over her shoulder, she added, "Jeffrey's going to be there too. Never let it be said that when I have a dinner, I have one everyone knows will be dull."

He couldn't help it—he laughed, and laughed harder as she nearly pitched herself into the bushes at the side of the road when she looked over her shoulder and raised a mock fist. Then he hurried into the house, passing through the long front hall into the kitchen where Mrs. Karragan was at the sink. She was as short as her husband was tall, round as he was sturdy, and with her faintly greying brown hair, just as youthful until one saw the lines about her eyes.

Knowing he was in for it, he hastily explained the impulsive dinner invitation, asked her to lay it on as best time would permit, and ignored her complaints about his constant changes of plans that generally required her to be both cook and magician.

Life in the Vicar house wouldn't be right unless she raised the roof about something at least once a day. As she had the evening he'd returned from the Brass Ring where he'd met Peter Reskin with a check that was exchanged for the artifact Jeffrey now wanted so badly.

It was a shallow wooden bowl, its painted designs faded, its purpose unknown though the partial figures and hieroglyphics around its border seemed to indicate something of a ceremonial nature. Nevertheless, from his first sight of it he'd thought it beautiful in its simplicity, and inspiring in its age, and had immediately cleared a space on the mantel for it.

Mrs. Karragan told him she could do better at Crenshaw's and for less than half the price.

When he had grinned and told her the artisan who'd made this was far more likely to have his work around in another millennium than anything Oliver Crenshaw could fashion, she'd begun her tirade, not the least part of which was a stiff reminder that the silversmith was her cousin, twice removed.

In his bedroom he threw off his sweater, kicked off his shoes, and stood for an indecisive moment at the foot of the bed. It was too soon to dress for dinner; he still had almost four hours.

Time enough however, he told himself, to begin du Maurier's book about the mesmerist, Svengali, or do the figures on the proposal Turnbell had made about investing in the village's telephone system. The banker had advised against it; there were only, he'd warned, ten thousand or so subscribers in the entire country, and he didn't see the situation changing anytime soon. On the other hand, Turnbell had also been opposed to purchasing the livery and would probably never own a motor car, electric or gasoline-powered, in what remained of his life.

Jeffrey.

He scowled at himself.

But the name wouldn't be banished.

And it occurred to him suddenly that there had to be, there must be items of equal if not superior value in Isle Hall that the young man could sell. Why, then, did he insist on having the bowl? Or Edmunds' gold statuette of the jackal-headed man? Or Turnbell's scarab?

A fist rose to his cheek as he groaned aloud in frustration. He was making all this so confusing, pretty soon he wouldn't be able to make sense of himself. And he felt worse when Karragan returned with Jeffrey's regrets; now he would have to wait until tomorrow, because Isle's departure from High Street today had made it rather clear that a surprise visit from John would be decidedly unwelcome.

"Damn!" he said. "Why the hell don't you just give him the money and be done with it."

Chapter 5

The night was filled with noise-leaves rubbing harshly like the palms of a crone, branches creaking like the knees of an old man, the woodland's nocturnal creatures foraging among the trees for midnight prey; the cry of a train, the rush of a stream, the stamp of an anxious horse against a stout stable door.

Noises unheard in the room made of stone whose color was once white, now darkening with age and the dust that filtered down from the hair-cracks in the ceiling. It was just barely large enough for the banded wooden chest squatting beside the door, the brass-and-copper brazier in the center of the floor, and the huge stone cabinet against the far wall.

There was smoke in the air, sharp with incense, turning upon itself and casting its own ribboned shadows on the darkly damp walls and over the figures painted there, in· rows, in columns.

On a stone table beside the cabinet was a shallow wooden bowl whose bottom had been burned black, a slender gold statuette of a jackal-headed man, and a scarab ringed with pearls. In the center lay a gleaming white robe with silver trim at the neckline, the ends of the billowing sleeves, and at the hem where the silver was intricately twined with gold.

And set apart from them all, near the table's corner, a small bronze chest encrusted with gems that sparked and flared in the light of the fire that burned low in the brazier.

When the door opened, the flames leaned away; when the door closed, the fire sighed and the embers brightened.

The man dropped his suit jacket on the floor, kicked off his shoes, pulled off his socks.

His face, though dark and smooth, was nonetheless weary, and dark eyes blinked against the smoke and stinging incense; the lips tightened, the jaw steadied. It was a mask of grim purpose, and only when the rest of his clothes were in a huddle by the door did he permit himself a smile that chased the weariness away.

He put on the robe, muttering to himself; he touched the head of the jackal, muttering to himself in a cadence monotonic; he opened the small chest with a small key from a chain bound to his left wrist and pulled out a necklace he slipped over his head, adjusting the sweep of tiny emerald skulls and tinier silver ankhs over the white silk across his chest.

He lifted the bowl and brought it to the fire, placing it on a wired stand that kept it away from the flames.

Then he turned to the north wall and stretched out his hands.

The cabinet doors swung open.

Inside there were stairs that led upward into darkness; and down them crawled the night's mist and the dim glow of the moon.

The man didn't hesitate; he spread his fingers, bowed his head, and waited.

The night was filled with noise that made the small cottage a few yards west of the rail line seem smaller and colder and less a place of solitary enjoyment than a place of isolation. The trees that flanked it on three of its clapboard sides grew higher as daylight fled, grew darker as the clouds rolled, grew fingers that clawed and hands that grasped and throats that sounded like the harsh laugh of a demon.

The Long Night of the Grave

And just after sunset, the wind.

Always the wind that rolled across the fields and slammed into the woods, bending new branches and shredding new leaves and passing over the chimney like the baying of a hound.

In the front room, whose walls were lined and stacked with books and journals, Peter Reskin knelt at the hearth, ignoring the wind as he tried to stoke the fire into giving him a comforting heat he had sorely missed while hiding in the forest just north of the village. Hiding until he had known it was useless and had taken the risk of returning, if only to feel the warmth once again.

Now if only he could find where he had lost youth and hope.

The flames spoke to him, and he held out his palms, sighing in the heat he hadn't really felt in almost ten years. He had been a young man then, just out of his twenties and feeling the power that knowledge had given him, feeling his way through a world the rest of the world didn't know existed.

Now he was just gone forty, and he never looked in mirrors because he didn't know the old man on the other side of the glass.

A stick hand held the poker, stick legs held him up, and the flesh across his cheeks was tight and growing tighter as the flames bellowed toward the flue. Perspiration drenched his face, the skin reddening from the heat, yet he stabbed at the logs and threw on more kindling and grunted when a spark flew to his wrist and scorched him.

The poker fell.

He lowered his head. Turned it slowly so he could see over his shoulder, to a shadow of himself rising and falling and filling the front hall and hiding the door. He turned back to the fire and covered his face with his hands.

Trying to remember the words that he needed to keep the nightmares away.

The wind rattled the panes.

The fire reached for the chimney.

And the words wouldn't be found.

Though his lips moved and his hands dropped away to knead at his thighs and his gaze followed the writhing of the flames, the words wouldn't be found.

A dog howled, and he scrambled back, fell onto his side, fought his way to his feet and stood trembling, looking out of the window on the other side of the room. To the silverwhite of the valley and the black wall of the hills; nearer, to the gleaming of the railroad tracks and the front yard whose grass had been barred with tree shadows.

The dog howled again, and he closed his eyes tightly.

It's only Gert Naysmith's hound, he told himself; on the loose again in spite of the warnings he'd given the old woman. He didn't care that she was his only neighbor; he'd never had use for her and her nosy ways, the way she looked at him as if he'd grown a second head every time he strolled past her hut just a hundred yards through the trees, up the line.

A third time, high-pitched and anxious.

He licked his lips, wiped his face with a sleeve, and moved closer to the sill. His reflection a ghost of a man once great with weight, once distinguished with fine clothes and a fine head of grey hair. A stickman now, hair matted and stringy, clothes dusty and torn, the face of a dead man whose last breath was a scream.

He blinked, and through his reflection saw a figure in the yard, dust swirling around him, not touching him, passing on.

"Oh my god," he whispered, and backed away denying.

A look to the hearth, to the flames, and finally to the poker aimed toward the embers. He snatched it up and hugged it. A wild look side to side. An idea that running out the back door and into the woods would save him, if only he'd be able to run all the way to the village through the dark.

Or make it to that damnable house of traitors where he knew the words were, written by his own hand between dark leather covers, on fine gold-edged paper; words that had once been his sword to keep his treasure from being stolen, a sword now aimed at the soft hollow of his throat.

He could do it. He had to do it—he was tired of running when there was no place to go.

Slowly he made his way to the window again and peered out from the side. The figure was gone. The wind had died. Nothing left but the moon, and a few strands of mist that became cloud over the tracks.

A tremulous smile, a shake of his head, and he turned his back on the outside. "They wouldn't dare," he told himself.

A nod of agreement, and he leaned the poker against the sill and hurried to the sideboard to pour himself a large snifter of brandy from an open decanter already half empty though it had been filled just that morning. He drank it in two large gulps, put a hand to his chest to feel the fire, poured himself another and carried it over to the hearth.

He never should have left the book out of his sight. That had been his second mistake. The first had been to let the others know he had it.

Damn, he thought, and drained the glass in haste. Brandy slipped over his chin, and he wiped it away with a sleeve, took a deep breath and strode boldly back to the window.

Nothing.

The yard was empty.

And filled with sudden anger he whirled and threw the snifter into the fire and went into the hall where he grabbed his coat from the rack, and screamed when something pounded against the door.

The coat fell to the floor as he backed out of the foyer, stumbling over a shadow, groping for the poker until it was safely in his hands.

The pounding again, and a panel splintered.

They couldn't have done it, he thought as he looked desperately around the room; they couldn't have, they need *me!*

The hinges snapped in thunder, the door fell inward, and something came in.

Reskin held the poker high as he sidestepped toward the dining room, chest rising and falling as though his lungs couldn't get the air that he needed.

The fire roared.

The wind rose again.

And it stood in the doorway, blackshadow and tall, the mist snaking in after it, bringing in the cold.

A moment of courage: "Go!" he commanded. "This is not your place, go!"

It didn't move.

Blackshadow, without a sound.

Reskin glanced at the wall beside him, cursing the day he'd pulled out the telephone to keep it from bothering him while he was trying to work; he glanced at the window and wondered if he could reach it before the blackshadow reached him; he felt the fire at his back and the brandy in his stomach, and courage fled as the first tear worked its way from a squinting bloodshot eye.

The thing was moving toward him.

One step at a time.

Mist curling now around its legs.

Blackshadow without eyes.

"No," Reskin whispered.

The Long Night of the Grave

Into the room where the fire gave it a face.

"No!" Reskin screamed, threw the poker as hard as he could at its head, and bolted into the small dining room.

A stack of books in his way, and he tried to dodge it, fell over it, and whimpered as he half-crawled, half-ran toward the kitchen door, his left shoulder striking the leg of the table, his right shoulder smashing into the wall when he tried to right himself and lost his balance.

A single glance behind, and he saw it framed by the window and lighted by the fire, nearly seven feet tall and looking like the grave.

He grabbed his arm and ran on, right, into the kitchen and out the back door without bothering to slam it shut behind him.

The backyard was shallow, and in six long strides he was into the trees.

And hadn't gone six paces more when he slammed into a bole and was knocked to the damp ground. He groaned and pushed himself slowly to his knees. His arm was afire, his chest felt crushed, and when he blinked and squinted into the night he could feel blood on his brow, slipping around to his right temple.

Dizziness as he staggered to his feet, swaying, turning without wanting to, and seeing the figure standing by him.

Blackshadow.

Waiting.

"Please," he whispered. "I didn't tell. Please, dear God, I didn't tell, I swear it."

The thing reached out its hand.

"Please."

And took hold of Reskin's throat.

The dog howled, and Gert Naysmith stormed angrily out of the house, a broom in her hand. She wasn't going to get a god's luck worth of sleep tonight if that misbegotten creature didn't shut its mouth. A look around the ragged yard, and she stalked to the tracks where the trees couldn't hide the face of the moon, but she still couldn't see where that idiot hound had gone.

Were it the rabbit sound she'd heard, or the raccoon, she could have let it be; she could sleep to that noise, God knew.

But not this one.

This was a hunting sound like none she'd ever heard, and she yanked at a trailing end of her shawl as she made her way south along the ties, muttering, wishing she'd given the beast a name so she could call it to her and find out what the hell was going on.

Probably that damned Reskin again, beating the poor thing because it bothered his precious studying. A hundred times she'd been there since the fool had moved in, trying to get him to see that he needed someone to look after the place—look after him, if it come to it—so's he could do all that work he kept claiming he had to do. Jackass. Killing himself was what he was doing. Killing himself right next to her place and not giving a damn.

She swatted a cowering field mouse off the rails.

She felt the chilled night through the layers of skirts found in people's trash, the homespun blouse, the sweater, the shawl.

She swatted the air and slowed as she approached the cottage.

The hound bayed, softly, sadly, as if it was ready to die.

Too damn old for this stuff, she thought as she hurried on; I should be taking care of myself, not some fool dog. Then her temper began to rise as the trees fell away, flickering light from the professor's cottage reaching out to his lawn as if the building were on fire.

The Long Night of the Grave

It was his fault, she thought sourly; everything had been fine until he moved in. The nights had been quiet, no one bothered her, no one talked to her. Just the way she liked it.

Then everything had changed.

The nights were no longer quiet, they were silent.

Two of her dogs ran off, the hound the only one that stayed and that because it was too old to do much of anything but bark; her cats, she never knew how many because they came and they went, all disappeared. Not one by one; all at the same time.

And the noises. Quiet noises. Sneaking noises. Noises she couldn't hear once she started listening.

Even poor witless Freddy didn't visit her anymore. He was ascared, he said, of the spooks and the haunts that he claimed had come to live in the woods.

Gert didn't know how, but she knew it was Reskin's fault.

And tonight, for some reason, was the last straw.

It was by God the last night she'd put up with him, hurting her pets.

With her broom at the ready, her dander up and running, she lifted one foot up to step over the rail and march at him and demand he stop whatever it was and leave her alone.

It took her a moment to see through her anger, but when she could, she saw the hound lying on its side in the slow-moving mist, and the thing coming toward her. One step at a time.

She threw the broom and turned to run, her foot snagging in a gap between tie and gravel. And when she fell, the side of her head struck the flat of the rail, and the last thing she heard was something stepping up beside her.

Chapter 6

The clouds joined after midnight, the storm hovering on wings of black and grey, sending wind down the streets to spin leaves into the gutters, sending droplets against windows to streak with the dust blown from the roads; hovering, and calling both wind and rain back when the sun rose and the clouds lightened and those who left their homes glanced back over their shoulders, sure they had seen something, telling themselves it was only the weather.

On Williamston Pike, John scowled at the dismal look of the back garden from his bedroom window. The flowers were dull, the grass lifeless despite the predawn shower, and the trees at the back looked no better than they did when autumn stripped them bare. Yet Leo was still out there each time the rain stopped, attacking the weeds, raking the leaves, pretending that what he did wasn't futile, wasn't dumb.

"God, Johnny," he muttered, "you're going to slit your throat next."

A palm wearily rubbed across his forehead.

He hadn't slept well; there had been dreams.

Not his frugal father chiding him for letting the family's slim cache of money slip away. Not this time.

This time it was shadowy figures passing a wooden bowl among them, something gold flaring back in a corner, and voices that slipped past his ear without leaving words behind.

The Long Night of the Grave

He had awakened twice with a start, each time staring at the bedroom door and swearing to himself that the glass knob was turning over, each time taking more than a few minutes to lie back among the pillows and stare blindly at the black ceiling until sleep took him again.

And brought back the dreams.

He knew it was because he was feeling guilty about Jeffrey, and knew too it meant he was weakening. If he couldn't shake the feeling, sooner or later he would go up to the Hall and tell Isle that the money was his, goddamnit, and don't disappoint me this time or it'll surely be the end.

He dressed slowly, leaving off his collar, pulling on a pair of trousers he used when hiking through the woods. A belt instead of suspenders. His lightweight blue sweater. Full boots instead of Wellingtons. This kind of weather, and the mood he was in, didn't deserve a proper outfit; and if he hadn't been afraid of tempting the dreams, he would have slipped back under the covers and let sleep kill the day.

Then he returned to the window and, holding the draperies aside, stared at the garden again, watching with melancholy envy as Karragan knelt on the damp earth and pulled out the weeds, lips moving, head bobbing, hands in a rhythm that knew each of the beds as if they were his children.

He was still standing there at ten o'clock when Mrs. Karragan knocked on his door and told him there was a visitor.

"At this hour, who?" he asked, following the plump woman along the hall to the stairs.

"He wouldn't give his name, and it's not for me to ask," she said stiffly. "A foreign gentleman is all I know."

He grinned at her disapproving back. "Bring him into the study, if you please, Mrs. Karragan. And some tea as well. I still don't think I'm awake yet."

She grunted a scolding at the hours he kept and headed for the door while he turned to the right at the foot of the staircase and hurried down the short hall to the first door on the left. He went in, threw open the drapes, and grimaced when the grey light didn't make the cluttered room look any better.

He had just managed to dump a stack of books from a leather chair when a knock on the doorframe turned him around.

Mrs. Karragan stood stiffly on the threshold, stern-faced and silent, then sniffed and backed away and a man took her place, without coat and hat, only a scarf thrown around his neck.

"Mr. Vicar, please?"

John managed a smile. "Do come in, sir." He hesitated. "You must be Khirhal Bey." He hesitated again before adding, by way of explanation, "Jeffrey Isle is a friend of mine."

The man in the severe black suit bowed slightly. His hair was black and brushed straight back over his scalp; his skin dark, his figure slender, his features soft with youth though there were harsh lines about his mouth, deeper ones at his eyes. He bowed again when John offered him the chair, and was ready to sit when Mrs. Karragan entered with the tray. John took it from her with thanks and closed the door behind her.

"Tea?" he asked.

Khirhal Bey shook his head.

John poured his own, sipped at it, winced with a smile, and drained the cup.

The man said nothing.

John sighed to himself, refilled his cup and sat on the corner of an open roll top desk. From the expression on the man's face, he knew pleasantries were going to be out of the question.

"To what do I owe the pleasure, Mr. Bey?"

The Long Night of the Grave

The Egyptian was perched rigidly on the edge of the cushion, hands flat on his knees. "You have, I believe, a certain bowl, Mr. Vicar," he said, the words clipped, the accent a cross between British and something John couldn't place. "I believe it was given to you by a certain Peter Reskin."

"Not given," he corrected politely. "I purchased it."

Bey lifted a hand: *a mere detail, no matter.*

"I should like to have it back."

An eyebrow lifted. "Ah. It's yours then?" And: damn you, Jeff, I was right—it's been stolen.

"My people's, Mr. Vicar, not mine alone. In this capacity I merely act as their agent."

"I see. You're from the Egyptian government, I take it."

"Not exactly," the man replied. "An agent merely of my people."

John waited for further explanation as he stirred sugar into the tea. There was something about the man he instantly disliked, a bearing that told him Bey considered him somewhat inferior, definitely less than an equal.

And when the man said nothing more, he cleared his throat. "And you are prepared to buy it back from me, is that it? Is that what Jeffrey suggested?"

Bey's lips, dark and full, twitched in a brief smile. "I have no intention of giving gold for what is rightfully ours, Mr. Vicar."

He smiled back as he placed cup and saucer on the desk beside him. "Well, that's something you'll have to take up with Mr. Isle, I'm afraid. You see, matters are a bit more complicated here than you may be aware of."

"Sakhtu," said Bey sharply.

John was puzzled. "I beg your pardon?"

The Egyptian rose to his feet, hands tight at his sides. "You see, Mr. Vicar? You do not recognize the name, yet you steal from him without qualm."

"Just a minute," he said, standing as well. "You'd better think twice before accusing a man of theft in his own home."

The man's chest rose and fell several times before at last he lowered his eyes. "I am sorry. It is my curse that my youth has not yet granted me patience."

John lifted a shoulder in a shrug. "Mine as well, Mr. Bey. But perhaps you'd better explain—"

Khirhal Bey folded his hands professorially before him. "Yes. Yes, thank you. Knowledge is always best for illumination of wrongs."

John barely managed to keep himself from frowning.

"Sakhtu," the Egyptian continued, "is a great priest, Mr. Vicar. A man of vision and unlimited wisdom. A man of power. During the heathen reign of Mentuhotep many centuries ago, he was severely persecuted for his beliefs, much as your ancestors were before they fled to this grand country." He looked up, dark eyes bright with what John thought were tears. "He is a priest of the great Ra, and at the time of Mentuhotep and Osiris, that was an invitation to murder. There is little left of him now, sir, save a few paltry artifacts to console those who follow him even unto this day."

"I see," John said. "And what you're saying is, Reskin stole some of these things from you."

Bey nodded once.

John moved to the window and once again looked out at his garden. His hands were curled just shy of fists in his pockets, and he wished he could put them around Isle's neck for getting him, and no doubt the others, into this awkward situation. His initial impulse was to give the bowl to the man and be done

with it. He certainly didn't need trouble with any possible fanatical followers of a long dead priest.

But though Bey was clearly sincere, there was something about what he'd just heard that didn't ring quite true, and he frowned briefly in a futile attempt to grab hold of it for a closer look.

"The bowl, Mr. Vicar," Bey said in a clear demand, impatience coloring his voice.

John turned. "No," he answered with courteous regret.

The young Egyptian recoiled as if struck. "But I have told you—"

"Yes, you have," he said quickly. "And so has Reskin told me something, and so has Mr. Isle. All of it different. I think, for my own peace of mind, I should speak with Edmunds and Thornbell first, don't you agree? After all, Mr. Bey, you expect me to take your word—forgive me, but a stranger's word—for something I do not yet know anything about. Would you, if you were in my position?"

Though the man's expression was impassive, the answer was clear in the slight narrowing of his eyes. Yet he did not argue; he merely bowed his head in acquiescence and followed John to the front door, looking neither left nor right until he was standing on the porch. Then he turned and seemed to grow taller in his dark indignation.

The wind had risen again; a scurry of leaves across the lawn, a scratch of shrubbery against the house.

"I would speak to them soon, Mr. Vicar," he said. "Very soon."

John leaned against the jamb. "I sense a threat, Mr. Bey."

"I do not threaten. I am only an agent."

And without explanation, he strode down the walk to the wall, hesitated, then turned left and disappeared behind the reach of the shrubs.

Slowly John pulled his hands from his pockets and forced them to open, forced his temper down, and told himself it would not be a good idea to chase after the man and beat him senseless for his arrogance. Whether the Egyptian had legitimate claim or not, no one was going to issue threats in his house.

"Wonderful," he muttered then. "Wonderful."

And saw Betty ride past on a high-prancing grey, waving to him as she headed toward the valley. He waved back half-heartedly and had just closed the door behind him when he heard Mrs. Karragan scream.

———

Freddy Jones didn't like the woods anymore. The trees were always trying to grab him, the rocks were always trying to trip him, and the invisible monsters that lived deep in the ground were always trying to eat him. They never had before. They had always run away when he came by, but not anymore. Not since a long time ago when that mean man took over the house by Aunt Gert's.

But today he had to face them. He had to see his Aunt Gert because he had to tell her what had happened the afternoon before, while he was at work, keeping the cemetery clean, just like he was supposed to.

It was terrible.

He was just raking the leaves when suddenly a dark man had come up behind him. When he turned, so scared he almost cried, the man put a coin in his hand and had spoken to him so softly he hadn't been able to move. And when he came back from wherever he had gone in his mind, they were gone.

He looked and looked, but they were gone, and he couldn't see what they had done. He didn't say anything to Mr. Emmett

46

the caretaker because he didn't want. to get in trouble. And it wouldn't have bothered him if it hadn't been for the dreams. All those terrible dreams about monsters and dying and strange people in strange clothes, dreams that made him cry most of the night.

And that morning when he came to work and started raking the graves near the back of the Park, he remembered the dark man and remembered the terrible dreams, and he had lost his breakfast right there on the ground, and then he had run away because he knew that if he didn't, someone would see him and blame him. They would say it was dumb old Freddy who let those people in, dumb old Freddy who let them in where they didn't belong.

People whose faces he couldn't even remember.

And he knew what they would say then: dumb old Freddy, time to lock him away.

His old coat flapped against his legs. His scarf was pulled high over a lop-sided face webbed with tiny scars, showing only the eyes, giving him the only disguise he could think of so they wouldn't take him to jail.

He ran the secret way, up the steep hill behind the graveyard and over the wall at a place where an oak tree had died and fallen against it. Through the woods that didn't like him anymore. Hiding behind rocks when he thought he heard voices; jumping into a dry creek bed when he thought he heard someone chasing him.

He ran as hard as he could until he reached the place where the railroad tracks began the climb over the hill. He thought maybe he should cross over them and hide in the mine shaft no one used anymore. But it was too dark there, so he headed south along the rails, waiting a very long time in the bushes where the Pike crossed over, shaking and whimpering and nearly crying out when a lady on a beautiful big horse rode over the tracks to the road on the other side. She didn't look very happy. He hoped she wasn't sad. But there was nothing he could do to cheer her up now because he had to get to Aunt Gert's before the rain came.

So when the lady was far away, he ran, as hard as he could.

And when he tripped and fell, he said all the bad words he knew because it hurt and he was stupid.

And when he looked up and saw what was left of Aunt Gert sprawled on the rails in front of him, he acted just like a little boy.

Freddy Jones screamed.

Chapter 7

Mary Karragan screamed.

She was in the kitchen polishing the crystal, and had gone to the sink to get herself a glass of water. A gust of wind slapped a snakelike branch of forsythia across the window over the sink, and when she'd looked up, startled, she saw a face staring in at her, eyes in a squint, stringy hair poking out from beneath a black bowler.

She backed away, threw up her hands and screamed again when the face vanished just as John raced in from the foyer and demanded to know what was wrong. A trembling finger pointed at the window, and he flung open the back door, reached around the jamb, and grabbed a brown suited man by the shoulder.

In a single motion the man was inside, Mrs. Karragan was reaching for one of the long knives hanging from the board over the counter, and John was angrily slapping the man's hat from his head.

"Cab," he said, "what the hell are you doing, sneaking around here like that? You scared the woman half to death, for crying out loud."

The little man snatched up his bowler and dusted its crown. "Sorry," Cab Planter said sullenly.

"And what's wrong with the front that you had to come around here," he demanded.

"I saw you were busy with that foreign guy. I thought I'd just come around here. I didn't mean anything."

"Right," he said. "Well, you're here. What do you want?"

"Came to get you."

Mrs. Karragan glared at him, the carving knife still in her hand. "Whatever for?" she snapped. "Mr. Vicar here hasn't got time to be fooling around with the likes of you, Cab Planter." She took a menacing step toward him, and he backed timidly away. "Out with you!" she ordered. "Out of this house before I do you for lunch."

John immediately pitied the pudgy policeman and gave his housekeeper a look that only made her scowl all the more.

"It ain't right," she said, standing her ground. "You got more important things to do than keep company with the likes of him. What would your father think?"

"He'd be pleased I wasn't getting in trouble," John said, waggling a hand behind him to send Planter around the table and out of the room. "Now I can't very well get in trouble talking with my friends on the force, can I?"

"It still ain't right."

"At least," he said as he backed toward the door himself, "let me hear what he has to say. It's only common courtesy."

"Common is right," she sniffed in disdain, and whirled when the back door opened and her husband came in, slapping at his livery to rid it of the dust the wind had taken to it. "And where have you been, Mr. Karragan, while I've been attacked and god knows what else?"

John left them to it and hurried up the corridor to the sitting room in front, where Planter was standing in front of one of the high windows, looking out at the brewing storm. He turned as John walked in and held his hat nervously in front of his chest.

"Sorry, Mr. Vicar. I didn't mean—"

The Long Night of the Grave

"That's okay," he said with a wave of his hand. "What's the problem, Cab? You don't look well at all."

Planter, jowls quivering as he turned his head side to side, cleared his throat several times before saying, "Freddy Jones."

"Oh good lord, what's he done now?"

"He hasn't done anything that we know of, except that he found his aunt, just a little while ago. She was on the tracks, down near that professor's cottage, that Reskin fella?"

John waited.

"She's dead, sir," the policeman continued. "Doc Gravell says she looks like she was hit by the midnight train." He shuddered. "He's right. It's an awful sight. Godawful mess."

"But why come to me?"

"It's Freddy. He says she wasn't hit by any train. He says she was killed by a monster."

John nearly laughed aloud, stopping himself when Planter refused to meet his gaze, and it didn't take long for him to realize the implication.

"No, absolutely not," he said sharply. "That's impossible. You've known Freddy as long as I have, Cab. He may be a bit feeble-minded, but he couldn't have taken the old woman's life. Jesus, he worshipped her. You know that."

Planter nodded miserably as he slipped on his bowler. "I know, I know. But I did some checking, and there wasn't a midnight train, nor has there been any this morning. There are repairs down the line."

"I see."

The detective sighed loudly. "Mr. Vicar—"

"Oh, for heaven's sake, Cab," he said with a smile, "how long do we have to know each other before you start calling me John?"

Planter looked shocked at first, then sighed in relief. "John it is, then." He managed a brief smile. "There's something else."

John waited.

"I went over to Reskin's place. To see if he'd heard or seen anything?"

"He's been gone for quite a while, I understand, Cab. Or so Jeffrey Isle tells me."

"So I've been told. He's surely gone now—his door's been smashed in, and the place is a shambles."

John shook his head slowly. "You've got yourself a mess there, Cab, no mistake about it."

The detective agreed. "And I don't mind telling you I'm stuck. Reskin I can deal with later. It's Gert I'm concerned with now. And I know it's early yet, we just finding her and all, but John, you should see her. She looks … she looks as if she was clubbed to death, and I'll be damned if I know how."

Part of him was ashamed for the excitement he felt, but his curiosity soon drowned that feeling. "No weapons?"

"I still have men searching, but so far, nothing." He held out a hand. "Look, I do wish you'd come with me. Freddy won't talk to anyone but you. And we can't get anywhere with him on our own."

John hesitated only long enough to know that the Karragans were still arguing back in the kitchen, a battle that would most likely last well into the night. With a nod to Planter he grabbed his topcoat from the rack near the door, snatched down a hat, and waited for him to join him.

Then, grabbing the detective's arm, he hurried down the walk to the closed police carriage waiting by the gate, and once seated inside, he pushed his hair out of his eyes and said, "You still have Freddy, I take it?"

"Yes sir. Miss Jerrard brought him in."

"What?"

"That's right. Seems she was coming back from checking her horses when she heard him yelling and crying. I don't know how she did it, but she got him to come in with her."

Amazing, he thought.

"Are they still there?"

Planter ducked from a leaf that seemed to aim at his eyes. "Miss Jerrard's left. But Freddy's still there. To be honest, we couldn't get him out of the station if we tried."

The carriage lurched forward, the black in the traces tossing its head anxiously as thunder once again rolled over the valley. Though a few minutes shy of noon, the morning was nearly dark enough for midnight, an unnatural shimmering dark that now and then brightened to silver as the clouds thinned, now and then shaded to an unnerving grey. Dust rose in spinning clouds along the roadside; leaves flailed at the driver; and the faster the carriage went, the more sudden gusts felt as if they were tipping the small vehicle over.

As they passed the entrance to the Avlock estate, he leaned past Planter and peered up the curving drive. Though the evergreens lining the drive were whip-snapped by the wind, he could see that nearly every window in the house was lighted, and a groom was trying to pull a pair of frightened greys toward the stable in back.

Then the trees took over again, and he slumped back.

The wind made conversation impossible, and he contented himself with wondering how Betty was, how she had taken seeing what was apparently a gruesome killing. He hoped then she hadn't left town; he had a feeling, nothing more, that seeing her would do him a lot more good than talking with Freddy Jones.

The wind paused.

The carriage plunged on through the shifting dark.

And the only sound was the rattle of the wheels, the crack of hooves, and the thunder answering them, without a flash of lightning.

———

Freddy was huddled as best his tall bulky frame would permit on a ladder-back chair in an office off the waiting room. His scarf was still wrapped about his face, his coat buttoned to the neck, and one hand kept raking his sodden hair away from his face.

When he saw John walk in, he leapt to his feet; when he saw Planter just behind, he fell back again with a groan and covered his eyes.

John looked to the policeman, who only tossed his hat on the scarred desk and sat behind it; then he grabbed the only other chair in the room and pulled it to him, turned it, and sat with his hands folded across the back.

"Well, Freddy," he said kindly, "what's all this I hear about you today?"

"I didn't do it, Mr. Vicar," Jones insisted, his voice catching, his eyes filling.

"I'm sure you didn't. And I don't think Mr. Planter here thinks so either." Freddy's expression was doubtful when he lowered his hands, but he pulled down the scarf just enough to free his mouth. "It was him."

A glance to Planter to keep him quiet; a smile for the obviously terrified man.

"Freddy, look, I know you've probably done this a hundred times already today, but why don't you tell Detective Planter and me what happened, all right? I won't say a word until you're finished, I promise. All you have to do is start from the beginning and don't leave anything out."

The Long Night of the Grave

"You'll laugh."

John put a palm against his chest. "I swear I will not. I give you my word."

And he waited patiently while Jones worked at his courage, his gaze darting from corner to corner, his eyes closing every time a clap of thunder shook the building.

"Yesterday I went to work," Freddy said then, whispering so softly Planter had to lean over the desk to hear him. "I do my work right, and I work hard because you got me the job and I don't want you get mad. Aunt Gert says I should be grateful for your help, and I am. I really am. So I got my things from Mr. Emmett's shed and I went right to work. I didn't stop for nothing. I took away all the dead flowers and all the dead leaves and I—"

"Jones, get to the point," Planter said impatiently.

Freddy started.

John warned the detective with a look and with a flick of his hand encouraged Jones to continue.

"Well, after them that came to put their loved ones away — that's what Mr. Emmett always calls them, their loved ones — after they went away, I went back to work. I don't like to work when there are prayers around. Aunt Gert always says that's disrespectful, and I'm not disrespectful of the dead, no sir, I'm not. So I did my work, Mr. Vicar. I did my work good."

———

John nodded, tilted his head as if listening harder, leaned back, leaned forward, and did nothing to stop the man from giving him a minute-by-minute account of his day, up until he'd left work and went to his room in the basement of the Brass Ring. Then he grew fearful again, pulling up his knees as if trying to curl into a ball.

And he began babbling.

He spoke of unseen monsters that chased him in his dreams, monsters in the woods that tried to eat him alive, and monsters in the cemetery that stalked him over the graves; he cried when he tried to explain how he'd found his aunt, and he cowered when thunder rattled the windowpane behind Planter.

"Freddy, get hold of yourself," the detective snapped when he could take it no longer. Jones froze, lower lip trembling, hands clasped about his knees.

In that moment John felt sorry for the policeman—the only account of a terrible event had to come from a man hysterical with fear and grief, a man who at the best of times had little use of his brain.

"Freddy," he said, over and over until Jones finally calmed down. "Freddy, can you ... did you see this monster?"

Planter snorted.

Jones nodded, then shook his head. "It was dark, Mr. Vicar. My dreams were really, really dark. I could hardly see him at all, but I knew he was there."

"But dreams aren't real, Freddy, you know that. They're just in your mind."

"I know."

"Well, then?"

Freddy gnawed at the tip of his thumb, his knuckle, looked over his shoulder at Planter, who was staring at him without expression. "When ... when I found Aunt Gert?"

John nodded, hoping the man knew that he understood the pain.

"I knew the monster had been there, Mr. Vicar. I knew it wasn't a dream."

They waited, only half-hearing voices at the front of the building, footsteps in the corridor outside the office.

"How, Freddy?" said John gently.

The Long Night of the Grave

"It smelled dead," Freddy whispered. Then he nodded once, hard. "I should know because I work there all the time. I'm not lying to you, Mr. Vicar. In my dreams and on the tracks, the monster smelled dead."

Chapter 8

As John moved down the steps to the pavement, he buttoned his coat and sighed. The brief surge of excitement he'd felt before reaching the station was gone, and now he was beginning to feel as dismal as the day was grey. Cab had obviously been expecting him to break through Freddy's absurd tale and expose the truth, and it hadn't happened. Now Freddy was in a cell, feeling betrayed, and he had no idea what, if anything, he could do about it.

His stomach growled.

He acknowledged the message with a lop-sided grin and, with a look at the sky and a prayer of thanks that the wind had calmed to little more than a stiff breeze, he decided to take his lunch at the Brass Ring.

The entrance was several doors off Centre Street, on Steuben Avenue. It was a small tavern only a handful of years old and, he suspected, not destined to last much longer than that since it could claim no regular clientele beyond those clerks and occasional laborers who used it for a quick glass before heading home at night; there was definitely no hope of competing with the Chancellor Inn for dining, offering little more than sandwiches at noon and bowls of pretzels and nuts the rest of the day; and more often than not the owner seemed disinclined to do much more than sweep a hasty broom over the uneven floor at the start of each drinking day.

The Long Night of the Grave

The narrow interior, bar on the right and tables on the left, was darkwood and dimlight, and when he found that the table nearest the window was empty, he took it, opened his coat and leaned back against the wall. And straightened so quickly he nearly fell out of the chair when he found himself staring into Betty Jerrard's face peering through the glass.

She laughed and came in, doffing her cloth cap and taking the chair opposite. "Well, this is hardly the place I'd expect you to be in," she said, shaking her head to smooth out her hair.

"And you, Miss Jerrard."

She giggled as she looked around her. "If Sterling could see me now, he'd kill me."

Then she stared until he cleared his throat with a swallow and beckoned to a weary, bone-thin woman who took their order and brought two tankards of ale right away.

"I like your outfit," he said after taking his first drink.

She was in a snug brown jacket with a white scarf loose around her neck, and a pair of trousers she wore when riding just to annoy her sister.

"Thank you," she said, turning side to side. "Sterling threatened to disown me if I left the house in it today."

"You left."

"I own the house," she said, and laughed, drank, put the tankard down and folded her hands around it. "Have you seen Freddy?"

He stared down at the foam and nodded, and needed no prodding to tell her what he'd heard that morning. Every so often he would look up, to see if she were affected or not, and each time felt himself more amazed. Most of the other women he knew would have been home by now, dousing themselves with salts and fueling their gossipy lives for at least the next six months.

Betty, on the other hand, was genuinely interested, and genuinely concerned. It was she, he knew, who had made sure Gert would find old clothes in the trash, and the odd parcel of carefully wrapped food.

He finished just as their sandwiches arrived, and with mutual grimaces of distaste, they ate. Quickly. Paying little heed to the odd looks they received from customers departing and entering. Ordering a second round of ale while John told her of his visit that morning, before Cab came to fetch him.

"But doesn't he have a right to the piece?" she asked.

"That's just it, I don't know. But as I told him, I can't just take his word that he's entitled to it. First, I have to get the truth from Jeffrey, and Reskin if he ever shows up again."

Her agreement was reluctant, but she said nothing more about it until after he'd paid the bill and they were outside, walking slowly along Centre Street, acutely aware now that their dress was markedly different than what was expected of them in public.

"We're horrible, you know," she said, taking his arm and hugging it to her side.

"Reprobates, at the very least."

And he smiled at her, liking the fact that she was nearly his own size, liking the way she never treated him like a fool save when he was being foolish. It was, he knew, trust. As Ned trusted his flashes of insight, she trusted his belief in the future.

So why, he asked himself, don't you propose and be done with it? She knows you're going to, one of these days. What, Johnny boy, are you waiting for?

The answer was simple: he simply didn't know.

"You know," she said as they reached Chancellor Avenue and started east, for the park, "it seems to me that you three are being awfully stubborn about this."

The Long Night of the Grave

A moment passed before he understood her. "Stubborn? I don't think so. Just careful, that's all."

"Are you sure you're not just trying to teach Jeffrey a lesson. At Khirhal Bey's expense, as it turns out?"

He would have argued no but an idle glance across the street made him stop. Frown. Look at her for so long that she frowned back and wanted to know what he was thinking.

"Gert," he said, taking her hand and guiding her through the traffic to the other side of Chancellor. "I'd like to know how the hell you can beat a woman to death without a weapon."

"No one said that," Betty told him. "They just couldn't find one."

"Well," he answered with a grin, "there's another way to find out."

The study at the end of the hall had only one key; not even the servants were permitted to enter. Its walls were covered with glass-fronted cases in which were displayed hundreds of relics of civilizations the owner had never seen, only read of. On its floor was a dark Persian rug. In the far corner was a writing desk, and a single chair sat by a small fireplace near the room's only window.

The lamp on the desk burned low.

When thunder sounded outside, here it was reduced to a low throated grumbling.

"You assured me there'd be no violence! I had your solemn word."

The speaker's voice was forcedly calm, and his face was hidden, only the rings on his fingers caught the light in green and amber fire.

"Alas, there is always violence of one sort or another. Life is not life without it."

"If we're found out—"

"We will not be. And if we are, who would believe it? You should not worry so much. It does not become you."

The draperies covering the window rippled as a draught slipped over the sill.

"I don't like it."

"It is not yours to like. It is yours to obey if this thing is to be done."

A grandfather clock sounded the sixth hour past noon, the chimes hollow, the echoes too long in the hallway beyond the closed door.

"I suppose … it was just an old woman after all."

"That is so. Just an old woman."

"Damn. And you're sure they won't know?"

"As sure as one can be, my love. I have done my best to learn what they know, but you must understand that I am not … how shall I put it? I am not one who can pass invisibly through your people. I must be careful. Extra caution is needed."

"I don't know why you just don't let me do it."

"If I am not invisible, what do you call yourself?"

"Well, I don't like it."

"You repeat yourself."

"Yes. Yes, I suppose I do."

Voices outside and the clatter of a carriage as it pulled under the portico.

"Darling, do you think we'll get them? I mean, will we succeed?"

"There is no reason not to think so."

"You sound doubtful."

"Nothing is ever certain."

"Christ, if they'd just stop playing at petty gods and give me the goddamn things, we wouldn't have to go through this!"

"Be calm, my love. What is, is. What was, cannot be altered."

The Long Night of the Grave

"Of course. Be calm. Just like that." A loud and deep breath. "And there is still no word from Peter. You're quite sure of that."

"Quite sure."

"You know, it's just possible that he panicked and left the country again."

"No. I don't think so."

The rings flared as the hands shifted nervously.

"Tell me the truth—is he still alive?"

"If I knew that, I would be a seer. I am not. I am only a servant and have only a servant's poor skills."

A short barking laugh.

The study door opened after a large key had been turned.

Murmuring from below and a woman's shrill laughter.

"I will see you at dinner on Friday, then?"

"Yes. I will be pleased if we are able to sit together this time."

"I have no control over that."

A gentle laugh, mocking.

"But you must listen to me—I will have no more violence, do you understand? I won't stand for it!"

"You are a pretty man, and a foolish one. Have you not yet learned that what you like and what you do not like are no longer of any importance. What is important is that we finish what is begun. And do not fool yourself—it has begun."

———

James Gravell's office was in a low, dark brick building on Chancellor Avenue, facing the park. The right half was his living quarters, the left half his surgery, and John counted himself lucky that the doctor was free when he rang the bell.

"John! Miss Jerrard!" Gravell said heartily. "What brings you two here?" The bearded and heavily paunched man took Betty's arm and brought her into the sitting room, John trailing. "Not under the weather, I hope. In this weather that could be fatal."

John laughed dutifully and stood behind a frail-looking chair Betty accepted. Then he glanced around the room all frills and fragile furniture and wondered how a man as large as Gravell could stand being in a place like this. He waited until the doctor eased himself onto a couch that wouldn't hold more than two rather thin children, then asked him about Gert Naysmith.

"Ah," Gravell said. "So that's it, eh? Playing detective again. And is Miss Jerrard your assistant?"

"Just giving him some help, that's all, Doctor."

Gravell sniffed, pulled a cigar from his jacket pocket and went through the ritual of sniff, roll, clip, and light without saying a word. Then, with the smoke clouding about his head, he closed his eyes.

"They told you she was beaten to death." A quick look then to Betty, who smiled prettily and assured him she wasn't going to swoon. After all, she was the one who had found Jones and the body.

"Well," the doctor said, somewhat disconcerted. "Well, you were told, then, about a beating."

"Yes," John said.

"I'm not so sure." The eyes opened, slowly. "John, I don't know how to explain it, but it looked to me as if she'd been trampled to death."

"On the tracks? James, come on."

"I know, I know, but that's what I saw. What the police choose to believe is their business."

The Long Night of the Grave

With a touch to Betty's shoulder, John moved to the high front window, staring out at the park's iron fence and the thick stand of trees beyond.

"You've examined the body closely?"

"Of course I have."

"No trace, then, of wood or whatever in her wounds?"

A loud series of puffs made John turn around. Gravell was staring at the ceiling, his expression one of indecision. He turned back just as the man said, "No. Not exactly."

An electric passed the building then, and two riders who were joking with the old man driving the motor car. He thought about Freddy. "James, see to it that Gert gets a decent burial, won't you? And send the bill to me."

Gravell answered with a grunt and pushed himself to his feet. "You're working for Jones, aren't you," he said, coming to stand beside him.

"In a way."

"Come with me, then. Both of you."

An exchange of shrugs as Betty rose, and they followed him into the surgery where, in a smaller room behind filled with glass-fronted cabinets of vials, instruments, and cartons of supplies, Gravell opened the drawer of a small desk and pulled out a tin box of the sort his wife probably used for buttons.

He opened it and held it out.

John looked a question at him, looked in, and saw lying on the bottom a strip of grey cloth tattered at the ends and edges, and flecked with dirt and dark stains. When he looked up, thoroughly puzzled, Gravell closed the tin again and placed it back in the drawer.]

"I found that under Gert's body," the doctor said.

"But surely the police—"

"Say it's a piece of her skirt."

"You don't think so, is that it?"

Charles L. Grant

"I think, John, I've never seen cloth like that in my life."

Chapter 9

Riding behind Betty on the already skittish grey was not something John enjoyed, despite the fact that it gave him a chance to put his arms around her without causing the entire village to turn red with indignation. They had left Gravell's immediately after the doctor admitted to the temptation to run tests on the mysterious cloth, and Betty, more than he, had convinced him to give in; then she told him she had to be home to dress for dinner, Sterling having invited Edmunds and Turnbell over for an evening's debate.

"Sounds lovely," he said. "Is this a trial run for Friday night?"

She glared but couldn't hold it, smiled and offered him the lift to his house.

At his gate he slid off, and was as surprised as she seemed to be when she leaned over and kissed him, and made him promise to be careful.

"Gert never harmed a soul in her life," she said then, "and she certainly had no valuables. There's something wrong, John, and I don't want you doing anything foolish."

And when she'd gone, he wondered how she'd known what he was thinking — that somehow Peter Reskin held the key to what was going on in the village. He had no idea if Naysmith's murder and Jeffrey's problems with the Egyptians were connected, but he told himself it wouldn't do a bit of harm to find out.

And the only way to do that would be to have a look at the bogus professor's cottage.

"You're an idiot, you know," he muttered several times later, when two hours of pacing aimlessly through the house had driven Mrs. Karragan to new anger, and himself to distraction.

"A complete idiot," as he saddled the roan just after six and walked her out to the road.

And he said it yet again when he reached the end of the Pike, and the sun had already slipped below the tops of the trees, scattered in the greylight between shadows, scattering shadows in wavering spears over the tracks. There was no path wide enough on this side of the line that would take him to Reskin's cottage, so he urged the horse over to Cross Valley Road and turned right, hunching his shoulders against the occasional gust of wind, squinting when a spray of sudden drizzle was blown into his face.

The clouds had separated out of their overcast and back into thunderheads that drifted across the sky, and in their passing left a chill that made his teeth chatter.

To the east he could see the outlines of distant farm buildings and smell the rich turned earth, the new crops, the lingering perfume of wildflowers dotting a fallow field; to the west, however, there was nothing but trees. The estates of Oxrun's wealthy didn't reach this far, and there were only a dozen or so scattered small homes to break the wall of dense woods.

The roan bobbed its head and snorted.

He steadied it with a soft word and peered into the shadows across the tracks, finally fixing on the clearing that marked Gert Naysmith's place. The house was hidden; and there was nothing but shadow left.

Not a sound but the wind's soft soughing.

The Long Night of the Grave

The roan skittered sideways, shying at something he couldn't see, and he leaned over its neck to speak to it again, stroking it, scratching it between its ears, and straightening when he came to Reskin's cottage. A quick survey of the land around, and he dismounted, leading the horse across the tracks and frowning when it tossed its head in protest.

"For heaven's sake, you're worse than Mrs. Karragan," he said, and wrapped the reins through a bush at the head of the clearing. The roan backed away immediately, its ears flat, its eyes wide and rolling. John held up his hands, his voice trying to be calming, but it reared without warning and pulled itself free. He yelled, leaping to one side when it charged him, then veered at the last moment and galloped back the way they had come.

"Well, I'll be," he said, hands on his hips. "You stupid ... do you know," he yelled then, "how far I'm going to have to walk, you stupid beast? Jesus!"

He kicked the ground angrily, yanked off his cap and raised a hand to throw it. Stopped. And shrugged. Walk he would have to do, but as long as he was here he might as well have a look around.

The trouble was, he thought glumly nearly thirty minutes later, there was nothing to see.

The yards front and back were empty; the house was closed up and the police, in an evident attempt to discourage looters and the curious, had nailed a new door on the front. The back entrance was locked. He'd tried peering in through the windows, but the gloom inside prevented him from seeing anything but his own weak reflection. And even when he managed to see past it, there was no sign of anything wrong. No sign of Peter Reskin. No sign of trouble.

He tried the front door again and swore at the police for being so damned efficient. Stepped back and glared at the roof.

Stepped back again and wondered how much trouble he'd get into if he broke a window. The answer was in there. He knew it. And though he supposed he could go to the stationhouse tomorrow and probably talk Cab into giving him a key, his curiosity was feeding impatience like dry brush.

He wanted to go in there now. While he was here.

The light drifted out of the air.

The clouds began to join to blot out the early stars.

A gust of wind made him pull up his collar, and he rubbed his chin against it thoughtfully.

When he took a third step backward his heel came up against a rock, and he pried it from the ground before he knew he had done it. But once done, he rushed around to the back and used it to smash through the pane on the door. Then he reached in and lifted the latch, shoved in the door and leapt inside.

A full minute passed before he was calm enough to move on, taking a box of matches from his coat pocket and lighting one, holding it over his head until, on a counter near the sink, he found an open box of candles.

It wasn't much, but it would suffice, and he moved swiftly into the front room and stood in its center, stood on the hearth, stood near the window and looked out at the yard.

It didn't make sense.

Someone had broken in by smashing down the door—why hadn't they simply broken a window as he had done?

Ash shifted in the fireplace as the wind slipped down the chimney, hissing, rasping, snaking around his ankles.

For a brief moment he could have sworn he wasn't alone; for a brief moment more he thought he heard footsteps outside.

He blew out the candle and waited, crouching in the corner between fireplace and front wall. Looking for shadows. Seeing instead the dark slide from the walls and cover the room as the clouds thickened outside and buried the moon.

There was thunder, and a faint flare of lightning behind Pointer Hill.

Finally, when he was positive it was only his imagination at work, he relit the candle and scanned the hundreds of volumes lining the walls, knelt and read the titles of those books stacked on the chairs and floor. Shaking his head; there was something wrong, something out of place. Moving on again, this time to the bedroom upstairs, where he discovered Reskin' s toilet articles still in the bathroom. In the tiny bedroom a search of the wardrobe and dresser produced nothing but an idea that wherever the man had gone, he hadn't taken any clothes.

Something wrong. Something missing.

The wind in the eaves.

"Damn," he muttered as he returned to the living room and stood by the mantel.

And "Damn," again when he realized what had been bothering him — though he'd come across a number of pens, full inkwells, and pencils during his look around, there were no notes left behind. No journals. No records at all of Reskin's far travels.

The only desk was in the corner by the dining room entrance, and it was as clean as if Reskin had just bought it.

He checked the books again, this time opening them at random and shaking their pages to see if anything fell out. He pulled the few sticks of furniture away from the walls, checked behind the few paintings, went through every drawer and cupboard in the kitchen; he tested the hearth for loose bricks, the mantel and desk for springs that would reveal hidden drawers or spaces; he returned to the bedroom and checked under the mattress.

And he was halfway down the stairs when someone tried to open the front door.

———

The doorknob turned slowly; a muffled thump as if whoever was outside had kicked the nailed door in pique.

Cautiously he moved down to the last step, wincing at each creak, holding his breath and briefly closing his eyes. His hand grabbed on the newel post in readiness to swing him around in case he had to run for the back, and he stared hard at the door as if he might see through the wood to the person on the other side.

Silence.

He let himself breathe freely and took the last step to the floor.

And swore silently when he glanced toward the back—if whoever it was out there went around to the kitchen, they would find the broken pane. They would get in. And he had no good explanation of why he was here.

The doorknob turned again, harder this time.

The urge to call out and tell whoever it was that the door was sealed was strong, yet something stayed him. The feeling of standing too close to ice. The scent of something just past ripe. None of it was real, but his hand remained on the post until he heard a weight shifting impatiently on the other side of the door. He broke from his standing and hurried as quietly as he could along the hall, praying he'd have the time to get out before he was spotted.

His foot came down on a piece of glass, and he stopped with one hand grasping the latch, listening until the knob rattled a third time. Then he eased open the door, closed it silently behind him, and dashed across the yard into the trees.

The Long Night of the Grave

A cloud split and the moonlight lay silver over the cottage and the grass, setting the windows deeper into the shadow.

He waited, crouched behind the stark trunk of a lightning-dead elm, the bark rough against his palms, his breath rasping no matter how hard he tried to keep it silent.

Thunder grumbled distantly to the south; the storm was finally moving off though the wind was rising again, snapping the higher branches and stirring the leaves on the ground.

The black behind him a weight on his shoulders, the cottage ahead shimmering when he found himself staring too long.

The wind grew damp.

He pulled his collar closer about his neck, about to dare leaving when he saw a pale shadow drift around the side of the cottage. Not very tall. Hooded. The hem of its cloak whispering over the grass. A single hand visible, holding the neck closed.

He stared so hard his eyes began to water, but the features he sought were invisible, and nothing about the shadow's movements suggested anyone he knew.

It stopped at the door, and he heard a quick gasp, saw it whirl around to stare at the dark woods. Then it was gone, light footsteps running, and he leaned against the tree with a silent sigh of relief, a slow shake of his head. It would do no good to run after it; even if he managed to learn who it was, he had no ready explanation for his own presence here. Yet he was pleased that someone else shared his interest in Peter Reskin; it confirmed his instinct and made him feel less the fool.

He waited ten minutes more, then, in case a third party should appear, before deciding to take a shortcut through the woods to the Pike. He wasn't afraid of getting lost despite the dark, and as long as he moved carefully neither would he embarrass himself by falling into a hollow and breaking a leg.

Fifteen minutes later, he began to wish he'd changed his mind.

The moon was inconsistent, and what light it did cast merely doubled the illusions his straining eyes provided. Twice he whacked his shoulder against trees he thought were shadows, and twice he stumbled into bushes because he'd sidestepped shadows he thought were trees.

Branches whipped at his face.

Nightbirds scolded him harshly.

The first clearing he reached was carpeted in mist that roiled and subsided like the surface of a boiling pot.

A twig snapped to his left; when he turned to face it, another snapped behind him.

Perspiration began to trickle down his spine and lay a sheen on his brow. He opened his coat and snapped down the collar, ordered himself to slow down, finally ordered himself to rest when a second clearing was reached, as filled with mist as the first, and as silent.

He leaned against a slender white birch and dried his face with a handkerchief, angry that he was unable to catch a clean breath, angrier still because he knew he was afraid.

With one hand still against the bole to steady himself he straightened and inhaled slowly, exhaled loudly, and saw a blackshadow figure standing across the way.

The mist rising behind it in spiderweb strands.

John didn't think twice.

He ran.

The direction didn't matter as he swerved to his right and ducked into the trees; all he wanted to do was get away from whatever it was that had come up on him so quietly, that stood there without moving, a giant of a figure so dark, so black, it seemed torn from the mist by a madman's hand.

Panic made him gulp for air though he wasn't moving that swiftly; panic tightened the movement of his heart and laced his ribs with stabbing pains; panic blurred his vision for only a

moment, but it was enough to prevent him from seeing the dead branch.

When it struck him full across the chest, he sprawled to the damp earth, rolled over, and groaned. Blinking rapidly. Hugging himself. Moaning as he fumbled to his knees, to his feet, and wiped sweat from his eyes ... and saw the body at his feet, twisted and broken, its face covered with dried blood and strands of shifting fog.

Its mouth was wide open in a perpetual scream, and its eyes were wide open and staring blindly at the dark.

"Oh my god," he gasped, and staggered on, kicking up puffs of ground fog behind him. An arm out to fend off the grasp of the underbrush, the other arm pressed against the ache where the branch had hit him.

Tripping over a section of rotted log and spinning around until he was stumbling backward, spinning again to dodge a thorn bush that tore through his jacket pocket, and righting himself in time to find a clear trail that led straight ahead.

Caution abandoned, he ran as fast as he could, thunder above him and thunder in his chest, until he broke out of the woods so suddenly he fell again, sprawling on the verge of Williamston Pike.

"Jesus," he said, pushing himself painfully to his feet once again.

A twig snapped.

A branch snapped.

A stone rolled to his feet and he looked up to see the blackshadow standing in the middle of the road.

Chapter 10

"It is my considered opinion," said Sterling Avlock, "that Mr. Cleveland ought to step down and let someone who knows what he's doing take this country out of its doldrums."

He was standing imperiously before a huge marble fireplace, the brick hearth two steps above the Oriental carpeting, the mahogany mantel nearly ten feet long. His high forehead and widow's peak added to the disdain that was his usual expression, and his left hand remained buried in his trouser pocket while the forefinger of his right constantly touched at and straightened his evening bow tie.

"A bit drastic, don't you think?" Sydney Edmunds said from his chair by the bow window. "Or are you secretly a Bryant man after all?"

Avlock glared at him and turned deliberately away, to smile at Howard Thornbell, seated on a brocade and velvet couch with Vera. "As a banker—"

"I bank," Thornbell returned with a cool smile. "And in the evenings, I relax. Sterling, for heaven's sake, I can talk to you anytime, but how often do I get to flirt with your wife? Please, let an old man have some pleasures before he dies."

Vera Avlock giggled, and Edmunds could not help but grin at the way Turnbell boldly eyed the woman's neckline. She was certainly suited for the fashion, he thought a bit wistfully, and vividly recalled the days when such exposure was relegated to a barmaid like Mazie Gorvern and the others who worked the lower class taverns.

And one would certainly never mistake this cavern of a room for a tavern. Paneling, oil portraits, two electric chandeliers, a half-dozen fringed carpets no doubt thumped twice a day, and all of it shrieking at the money in Avlock's private vault at the bank. Sterling did not believe in reticence when it came to spending on himself.

A brief argument broke out then over the wonders of the Chicago Exposition, which Sterling with thumb in patterned waistcoast applauded and Howard decried, and when Vera suggested that it wouldn't be long before things like Blue Ribbon Beer would bring the local drunks to the estate's very doors, it was the first time in ages Edmunds had seen the two men agree on anything.

Yet he knew it wouldn't last, and a brief glance at his watch made him wonder when the damned fool was going to give them a meal. Eight o'clock. It was going to be a long evening, he thought wearily; I ought to be home in my bed.

Then, with some effort, he rose when Betty came into the room holding Jeffrey Isle's arm. The young man had said barely a dozen words to either him or Howard since they'd arrived, but at least he was making small attempts to be civil.

He nodded; Isle nodded back and whispered something to Betty, who shrugged her nearly bare shoulders and left him, pointlessly announcing she would see about dinner.

Isle came over and stood beside him, and together they listened to Avlock denounce all who lived in Washington as liars and thieves, and perhaps it wasn't beyond the realm of possibility that standing for office from the Station might be in his future. Vera applauded politely, and Thornbell was forced from his examination of her prominent chest to respond that he'd probably sooner have Eugene Debs in the White House.

"It isn't going very well," Edmunds remarked quietly when Sterling drew himself up for a retort. Isle sipped at a glass of sherry. "What do you expect when the fool invites only a handful of people, and they don't much care for his company in the first place?"

"Then why did you accept?"

"My reasons," he said shortly. "And you?"

"I was intrigued," Edmunds confessed. "He's up to something, and I couldn't keep away."

Isle laughed silently, set his glass down on the broad sill behind them, and frowned. "I assumed John would be here," he said.

Edmunds raised an eyebrow. "So had I. Don't tell me you're worried, Jeffrey."

"Far from it, Sydney. Believe me, far from it."

Edmunds waited for the bitter remark, the caustic comment, and was surprised when there was none. For the past two years John and Jeffrey had been not quite announced rivals for Miss Jerrard's hand, and the way Isle had been behaving lately, such rivalry would ordinarily have blossomed into all-out war.

"Life," Sterling said then, slapping a hand on the mantel.

"Nonsense," Turnbell replied. "Isn't it nonsense, Syd?"

Edmunds, without having the slightest idea what was going on, lifted a hand to indicate he was unsure.

"Like hell," said Turnbell, and immediately apologized to Vera for his language. "How can you say that?"

"I didn't say anything," Edmunds answered.

"Because there is nothing to say," Sterling told them all. "The way to power and to wealth is through life itself. The longer you live, the more you have of both. And the most powerful man is the man who outlives his enemies and lives long enough to test and retest his friends." His smile was feral. "Isn't that right, Jeffrey?"

"Oh now really," Turnbell protested.

"No, it's all right," Isle said with a smile. "As a matter of fact, I quite agree. The question is, of course, who will do the living and who will do the dying."

"Precisely," Sterling said.

"Yes," said Isle softly, and Edmunds felt a chill that all but made him shudder.

At that point the butler stood in the entrance to announce the arrival of Yasfiera Bey.

And at the same time a woman screamed from deep within the house.

———

The cot in the cell was hard, lumpy, and Freddy couldn't stop rolling side to side in an effort to find comfort. This wasn't like he imagined jail would be at all, and though he didn't like the red-faced man who had come in to yell at him for making so much noise, he thought it was almost fun.

He wasn't a criminal. The little man in the brown suit told him that a lot after Mr. Vicar had left. But it might be a good idea, the detective had said, if Freddy stayed in a cell. Just for tonight. And in the morning he could go home.

He wasn't too sure about that.

He would have to go to work; he would have to go to that place that made him remember the dreams.

But maybe, he thought, if he didn't sleep he wouldn't dream; and if he didn't dream, tomorrow would be better and he wouldn't get in trouble with Mr. Emmett.

A good idea, Freddy, he told himself as he sat up against the wall; sometimes, you know, you're not so dumb after all.

———

In the stone room, a prayer, and the thunder returned. Fire danced, shadows crawled, and the jackal-headed man turned on its gold base to face the dark man kneeling in the center of the floor.

In the stone room, a keening, and in a high corner a spider withered and died.

Betty sagged for a moment against the door frame, swallowing dryly, then pressing a hand to her forehead before reaching out to grab John's arm and pull him inside. The kitchen staff had run to her when she'd screamed at the sudden sight of him in the doorway, and it took her several seconds to assure them she was neither being attacked nor was the house under siege. None looked convinced, but she held them off with a stern look and brought him into an empty side pantry where there was a sink and a stool. She made him sit while she opened a cupboard beneath the basin.

"I'm all right," he said quietly.

"You look terrible. I'm going to call a doctor," she said, holding a cloth under running cold water.

"No, please," he protested. "I'm all right, really. Just a little tired."

"Tired?" She looked askance at him. "You look as if you've been through a war, John."

If he looked the way he felt, he had no quarrel with her. A glance at his reflection in the mirror over the basin made him wince. His face was grimy and scratched, his hair clotted with dust, blades of grass, and slivers of leaves, his coat torn at the pocket and streaked with dirt. There was a bruise on the back of his right hand as he tried vainly to make some sense out of his hair, and the rest of him was just as bad.

"Hold still," she commanded as she began to clean his face. "Are you sure you're not hurt?"

His smile was painful. "Some banged up ribs, that's all."

The Long Night of the Grave

"John, what happened? You scared me to death."

"Then we're even," he told her lightly.

"It's not the same and you know it, John Vicar. Now hold still while I—"

Then Avlock and the other guests rushed into the kitchen, and Betty looked heavenward for strength.

"What in god's name is going on here?" her cousin demanded when he came to the pantry and saw what she was doing.

"I am nursing," she answered, winking at John, and wincing as he did when the cloth reopened a small cut beneath his eye.

John gave the man credit—when Avlock saw his condition he at least had the grace to gasp his shocked astonishment. A moment that lasted only until he realized there were no serious injuries.

"You choose an odd way to visit a neighbor uninvited," Avlock said in disgust.

"I didn't choose," he answered mildly. "I ran into a bit of trouble while I was riding. My horse threw me and decided to head back home. The Karragans have the night off, and this was closer, for me. I'm sorry if I disturbed you."

Avlock had no time to respond. Edmunds crowded him out of the doorway and was followed by Turnbell and Jeffrey Isle. There was someone else out there, but he couldn't see past the railroad man's girth, and as long as Betty insisted on treating him, he decided to let the questions wash over him, answering with grunts and nods until, at last, she deemed him presentable.

He stood slowly. The backs of his legs ached, and his ribs, yet he stubbornly refused to give Avlock the satisfaction of seeing him incapacitated. Not that it mattered; the man was already snorting in disgust at the attention Betty was giving him, and he noted that Jeffrey had left.

"Thanks, " he whispered as she took his arm and led him into the main kitchen. "I'd best be on my way."

"You'll do no such thing," she said. "If that place of yours is empty, then you'll stay here until you feel better. Besides, you look as if you could use a decent meal. And," she added quietly, so the others wouldn't hear, "I could use a decent explanation."

He shrugged; she pinched him.

"Betty, this is too much," Vera complained, looking him over without disguising her distaste. "He's not even dressed."

"He fell off a horse, for heaven's sake, Vera," she snapped. "He's lucky he hasn't broken his skull."

"Indeed," said Edmunds. "Then may I suggest a simple meal, a glass of light wine." He coughed to cover a grin. "In here, of course, Vera. We wouldn't want to disturb our own dinner."

Betty's sister still looked doubtful, but Edmunds took her arm and led her, chatting softly, out of the room. Thornbell left with no expression at all. And when they were alone, Betty brought him to a small round table in the corner by the door where she served him herself, all the while keeping the curious servants at bay.

And when she'd finished she sat, folded her arms over her chest and said, "Well?"

He began to tremble and couldn't stop it. He was cold. Gripping the edge of the table didn't help, nor did emptying the wine glass she'd placed before him. He was cold. Clenching his teeth only made his jaw ache, and though he attempted a smile for her sake, he knew his lips were quivering like a child ready to burst into tears.

"In a minute," he said when she rose anxiously. "Just … in a minute."

Which became five, and ten, before he was able to sit back and close his eyes.

"John, what is it?"

"I've found Reskin," he told her flatly. "He's dead. And if I'm not mistaken, it's the same as poor Gert."

At that moment he sensed someone else enter the room, and he looked to his right, past the wood-counter islands where the meals were prepared, to the door on the other side.

A woman stood there in a frilled and fluffed scarlet dress which seemed too much like blood against the dusky hue of her skin. Her hair was black and long, and hanging straight along her spine; her face so familiar that even had he not seen or heard of her before. he would have recognized her at once.

He stumbled to his feet.

Betty rose as well, and a glance showed him how displeased she was, a displeasure not restricted to a simple interruption.

"John," she said coolly, "may I present Yasfiera Bey. Her brother you have already met. I believe."

The woman drifted across the floor as John groped for the table and leaned against it. Her dark red lips were parted in a polite smile, but the black eyes were unmistakably and unrelentingly cold.

"Mr. Vicar," she said, holding out a hand he was constrained to take. "I am told you have had trouble this evening."

"Some," he admitted. "But I'm fine now."

Her smile widened. "For now, yes. But in my country things change. Sometimes, like the desert, they change rapidly."

He bowed. "I appreciate your concern. I shall be more careful in the future."

"You do that," she said, turning to walk away. "You do that, Mr. Vicar. But be careful of the night."

Chapter 11

The clock in the hallway struck the tenth hour.

He sat alone in his study, a single brass lamp burning under a green glass shade, a snifter of brandy beside his right hand. The draperies were open to let bars of moonlight fall on the carpet, and the wind that had shredded the clouds at last had fallen to a whisper.

The house was silent.

On the desk blotter was the wooden bowl, and he touched it with a finger, turned it slowly on its base and held up a magnifying glass to enlarge and distort the figures around its middle. A sip of brandy, another turn. A glance up at a book propped open behind the bowl, its pages rumpled from hasty turning, revealing now sketches of ceremonial items from desert tombs opened in the past eight years. The bowl was not one of them. Nor had he been able to find the name of the priest, Sakhtu, in any other book he owned.

be careful of the night

Betty had bridled at the implied threat, but he'd not said a word, passing it off as some sort of proverb, perhaps a blessing to protect him from further harm. She hadn't believed it; and neither had he, but as soon as he had left, by the back door, he'd sensed a change in the air not attributable to the passing storm—a lessening of tension, a return of true spring.

But he hadn't forgotten the blackshadow, and once home had called the station to tell them of Reskin's body. Planter had been roused at home and came out right away with several of his men, and they'd taken the carriage to the place on the Pike where John had broken free of the woods. With a lantern held high they moved along the path, deeper through the mist, until they found it.

The detective had thrown up; John merely directed the three officers with them to wrap the corpse in burlap and place it on the carriage rack. When Planter was able to speak again, John answered as many questions as he could, silently accepting a rebuke for breaking into the cottage and agreeing to come to the station in the morning to make a statement.

They parted shortly before midnight.

He said nothing of the blackshadow; Planter wouldn't have believed him.

And he sat in the study till an hour before dawn, staring at the bowl, turning it, touching it, waiting for something to tell him what was going on.

Trying not to remember what Freddy Jones had said about monsters.

be careful of the dark

Trying not to remember the odor he'd smelled when the blackshadow first rose out of the wind-twisted mist.

Waiting in the stone room.

Arms spread, eyes half closed, incense sharp and senses even sharper.

Watching the stairs for the blackshadow to come home.

———

Jake Emmett stood impatiently at the door of the workhouse with his hands on his broad hips. His bowler was already in place, a signal that the idiots who had worked late for him today had better be gone or they'd be locked in overnight and good riddance to them, one and all.

He snorted, turned his head, and spat a stream of tobacco juice contemptuously into the worn grass behind him.

Idiots. All the time he was saddled with idiots when all he ever asked for was a few good men to help with the raking and the cutting and the once-in-a-while digging. Of course men like John Vicar wouldn't know a goddamned thing about working with their hands, would they, what with all their money and fine clothes and what did they give a damn that he had to stand around every goddamn night waiting for drunken half-wits and idiots to find their damned tools they'd left behind during the day.

Fat lips in a humorless grin, he spat again, took off his new bowler and wiped a sleeve over the crown, slapped it on again and hoped to god the police kept Jones in jail forever. An old woman and a dimwit. No loss. She was always nosing around, and he was always getting lost, always late getting out. It never failed. Just when he was ready to set up with a good long drink and a better long woman, that fool would take the wrong turn and end up screaming for help.

Sometimes, on slow nights, it was funny; tonight, when he'd thought he'd been spared the wait, two of his men had forgotten to cover an open grave back by the Avlock mausoleum. Just his damned luck. He'd been trying to lift the barmaid's skirts for two months now, and she'd finally agreed to see him in his rooms. Two months after buying her drinks and watching her flirt with the others in the downstairs at the Inn.

And if those fools did him out, he was going to break their goddamn backs.

Like Jones, forever whining about people not belonging, about monsters and ghosts and Jesus Christ knew what else.

The Long Night of the Grave

"But he can't do nothing unless I stand over him," he'd complained only last week to that toffy Vicar, who you had to watch out for because he was so damned chummy with the cops. "For Christ's sake, sir, if you'll excuse me, he talks to the damned graves, for Christ's sake."

And Vicar had only smiled, patted his shoulder, and suggested that Emmett be a little more patient.

"Patient, my ass," he muttered, spitting, wiping his chin, and drawing himself up when he saw the men hurrying toward him out of the dark.

"What the goddamned hell kept you?" he bawled, holding his fat hand out for the key. "Don't you ever watch the damned time, you—"

And astonishment silenced him when one of them only threw the key at his chest and kept on going, full speed.

Emmett swiveled open-mouthed to watch them dash through the gates and turn right. The stone wall hid them, but the sounds of their running were as clear as the image of the woman he had waiting only ten minutes' stroll away.

"Well, I'll be damned," he said. "Well, I'll be damned."

Too startled to chase after them and demand an explanation, he ducked back into the shed, put the key into the safe behind his desk, and turned out the gaslight. Then he shrugged into his coat, settled the collar around his thick neck, and strode to the exit. The heavy gates squealed on their hinges as he pulled them closed, but as he worked the chain-and-lock through them he stopped, and wondered.

The idiots had run away. Jesus God, suppose they'd been snooping around and wrecked something back there, the Avlocks would have his head and his job. He wiped a damp hand over his face slowly, trying to decide if he should just let it be and play dumb if anything was wrong, or if he should take the time to check on it himself.

"The girl ain't gonna wait all night, Jake," he told himself.

But if them idiots had busted something, Jake Emmett wouldn't ever show up because he'd been skinned alive and hanging from some damned flagpole someplace.

"Hell," he muttered, and opened the gates just wide enough to let him squeeze through. Then he fetched a lantern from the shed, lit it, and rushed off along the paths he knew like the swollen veins on the backs of his hands.

Five minutes, he promised himself; ten tops, and he'd be on his way. She wouldn't even know he was late; and when he showed up with the gin, she wouldn't care.

The lantern swung at his side.

His shadow snapped forward and back across the path.

The nightwind rose and chased a leaf to his heels, shook the foliage, took a voice like a crone husking over a cauldron.

He glanced side to side, hating the way the granite and marble glowed in the dark, hating the way the sculptures on some graves took the dark to fill their blind eyes, took the shadows to give themselves movement.

Angels became demons.

Children became creatures with claws instead of hands.

Obelisks became swaying pyramids that leaned toward him and hid the moon.

Then the path straightened, and he was there.

By daylight the mausoleum was forbidding; after sunset it was forbidden. It stood by itself near the back of Memorial Park, just where the wooded hill rose to form the Station's northern boundary. A high iron fence set it off from the plots of the village's early dead, and outside the fence a tall screen of evergreens that kept it mostly in cool shadow. It was as large as a summer cottage, white marble and graven columns and a rose window over the entrance that lay triangles and squares of pale color on the white marble floor inside when sunlight managed to break through the thick needled boughs.

At night it glowed, the stone seeming to reflect the cold of the moon, casting its own shadows, growing rather than shrinking when the dark filled the air around it.

Jake sniffed, hesitated, then pulled and pushed at the gate, grunting his satisfaction when the lock didn't give.

He held the lantern high and tried to see if the fools had somehow managed to break the stained-glass window, but it seemed all right, and nothing lay on the path that led to the doors that looked, from here, as if they were shut tight. He scratched his forehead. If it was something inside, he wasn't going to worry about it. He definitely wasn't about to go all the way back just to fetch the key. If it was something inside, those idiots would pay for it in the morning.

A quick check around the outside, Jake, he told himself then; a quick check, m'boy, and the rest of the night's yours, look out, little Mazie, your Jake is coming home.

He chuckled, wiped a hand over his mouth, and pushed his way through the gap between the trees and the fence, keeping the lantern high and sighing his disgust when he saw nothing amiss by the time he'd reached the back. A fool's errand, and he chewed, spat, and nearly swallowed the tobacco when he saw a shadow standing near the tangle of vines and shrubs that covered the fence.

"Hey!" he said loudly.

The shadow turned toward him.

And his eyes widened when he saw someone else, a man in dark clothes standing inside the fence, near the mausoleum's blank rear wall.

"Jesus, what the hell are you guys doing here!'

Grave robbers, he realized then; they were going to break into the crypt and carry off what they could.

His eyes narrowed.

The shadow stepped forward; the dark man didn't move.

"All right, you sons of bitches," he growled, "you get your asses out of here, now, and I won't say nothing."

The shadow moved again.

"Just move on, get yourselves over the wall, and I won't call the cops, you got me?"

Into a fall of moonlight.

Jake gasped and dropped the lantern.

Only once before had he ever seen anything like it—a coffin dropped by its pallbearers, the lid springing open, the body spilling onto the ground, wrapped in a shroud so tight the dead man's face had been outlined in the cloth.

But that corpse had been fresh; this one looked a hundred years old.

He fumbled in his pocket for the cash he always carried, backing away, his throat filled with sand, his stomach filled with ice.

The shadow, blackshadow, reached out a hand swathed in grey cloth.

The dark man turned away and walked through the marble wall.

And Jake Emmett screamed as the hand took his throat and lifted him off the ground.

Chapter 12

Midafternoon, and the sky was overcast, the light wind damp, as John stood to one side of the mausoleum gates, hands deep in his pockets, his expression thoughtful as he watched two men in white carry Emmett's corpse on a stretcher down the path toward the Park exit, James Gravell walking solemnly behind them, not looking around when John called his name.

He shivered then at the day's chill and raised his topcoat collar high. He was tired, sand packing his eyes even though he rubbed them every few minutes. He'd been at the station giving his statement when the call came about the caretaker, and it hadn't been long before the Park was swarming with uniformed police, not a few of whom spent time in the shrubbery, losing their breakfasts and groaning.

John himself had tried to be as dispassionate as he could when he viewed the body, twisted and trampled beneath a young oak, but even now he knew he was still somewhat pale.

He took a deep breath to clean out his lungs, and turned as Cab came toward him.

"Every inch," the detective said glumly. "I've been over every inch of this damned place, and I can't find a thing." He looked up hopefully. "You?"

"Not a thing," John said with regret. "Gravell?" Cab snorted. "He says it's the same as the others, but hell, John, even I can see that. The question is—why? And who?"

He moved on with a sigh, calling his men to him and leading them away, while John stayed where he was, feeling the marble cold behind him, feeling the sky lowering overhead.

He turned to stare at the mausoleum, lower lip between his teeth.

There was a connection between the murders and the thing he had seen the night before, he knew it, he felt it, and the instinct Ned Stockton had relied on in the past told him it had to do with something in there. Behind those doors. Though he didn't know why.

The trouble was, Avlock had adamantly refused to permit anyone through the front gates except Cab Planter, and had done so only when the policeman threatened to talk to a judge. No one else had gone in. Planter had been satisfied with whatever he'd seen.

In there, John thought, and stiffened when he sensed someone standing behind him.

"A fortress," a woman's voice said.

He nodded, releasing a suddenly held breath. "I suppose you could say that, yes. Our version of the pyramids, I think."

Yasfiera Bey moved soundlessly to stand at his side. She wore a long, deep blue cloak, its hood up, the folds hiding her face. "And no less safe, Mr. Vicar. Thieves plunder our graves as well."

The tone of her voice made him glance at her, and look back. "Your brother has told you, then?"

She nodded.

"You disapprove of my reasons too, I assume."

"It is not my place to approve or not, Mr. Vicar," she said. "Khirhal does what he must."

He shivered again, violently, in a gust of the wind and drew his arms closer to his sides. "He will be at the Avlocks tomorrow?"

The Long Night of the Grave

"Yes."

"Well, then, so shall we all. Perhaps then something can be done to clear up this situation."

The woman turned to move away, and looked back over her shoulder. Her eyes were invisible, her red lips thin. "It will, Mr. Vicar. I'm sure of it. It will."

He stared after her for several minutes, until the gravestones and trees hid her from view. Then, with a shrug, he dismissed her and made his way to the back of the fence. The soft ground had been thoroughly trampled by the police and others, but he wasn't looking for footprints now; Emmett had returned here for a reason, presumably at the end of the day, and the workers who had left before him had not known why.

Knowing the slovenly caretaker as he did, John could not believe it had been a last minute check to be sure all was in order. He wasn't that conscientious. So there was another reason—a meeting, a reconnaissance, something. And an hour later he found part of the answer.

"Well," he said. "Well, well."

Three bars in the fence had been filed through and refitted so snugly that it would take more than casual effort to pull them out and pass through to the plot beyond. Grave robbers, he thought; Emmett might possibly have been part of a gang.

Once inside, he grunted and dropped carefully to his hands and knees, crawling along a path from the fence to the mausoleum's wall, shaking his head, sitting back every so often and stretching the stiffness from his neck and shoulders. By the time he reached the wall, the clouds had thickened and the light was nearly gone, but he'd found nothing, no sign of tunneling, no chisel marks in the stone; and when he walked around to the front and tried the gate and doors, they were securely locked.

The wind blew again, softly keening over the tomb, and he hurried back to the fence, passed through, and replaced the bars as he'd found them.

Dimlight, faint shadows, the tolling of a church bell.

He stood on the street beside his tethered roan and frowned, looked back at the graveyard and passed a hand over his face. Looked up at the sky and rolled his shoulders to banish the tension growing there, inhaled and exhaled while he counted to ten. Then he mounted the horse and rode down the street without seeing, without hearing, until he found himself in front of Dr. Gravell's house.

———

"I saw what I saw," John insisted. following the large man into the makeshift laboratory at the back of the building.

"You saw nothing a shadow couldn't do," Gravell insisted.

"It was no shadow."

The doctor said nothing. Instead, he opened a drawer in a cabinet and pulled out a small wooden box, flipped back the lid and stared into it. John stood beside him; it was the shard of cloth found beneath Gert's body. Next to it was another piece, longer and encrusted with black dirt.

"Today?" he asked quietly.

Gravell nodded.

"Do you know yet?"

"All I can tell you, John, is that it's old. Very old. A form of linen, I think, that should have been dust before you or I were born."

"Grave robbers," he said with a sharp nod. "I'd thought as much." Gravell took a pair of tweezers and gingerly lifted one of the pieces, held it up to the ceiling light and shook his head. "It's not part of a shroud."

"It has to be, James."

"And there have been no graves opened as far as I know."

Frustration clenched his fists. "So what are you saying? The killer was wearing whatever this is?"

The doctor looked over his shoulder. "You tell me, John. You tell me."

———————

Alden was behind the duty desk again and took obvious great pleasure in telling him that Jones had been released first thing that morning.

"Then where is he?" he demanded. "He wasn't at work."

"Not my job to know, is it," the sergeant said. "Maybe he's out thumping someone else."

John refrained from leaping over the railing, turned stiffly and marched out, trying to ignore the man's quiet derisive laughter. A moment on the station steps to find his composure again, and he hurried up to the Brass Ring, to a short flight of stone steps leading down to the service entrance on the far side of the tavern. The door was open; he walked in, and down a short stone corridor to a narrow door on the left.

He knocked, and held his breath when the door swung open.

The room was tiny, smelling of garbage and stale ale, liquor and urine. A cot on the righthand wall, a chest on the left, a rickety table with a lantern and a Bible beside the cot. There was no sign of Freddy, and when he asked the barman upstairs, he was told that the half-wit hadn't been seen since the day before.

On the street again he tapped his foot impatiently, unable to think of where the man might be. Hiding, he suspected; hiding from the monsters.

Retrieving his horse from in front of the police station, he rode out of the village toward home, changed his mind when he reached the wall, and hurried on. To Isle Hall. A massive brick building drowning in rustling ivy, its windows high and shuttered, all its chimneys giving smoke.

He dismounted and knocked on the door. Knocked again. Knocked a third time and stalked off in disgust around the corner. Through an unkempt yard where shrubbery grew wild, flowers were already dying, and stones poked through the ground to trip at the unwary.

There was no response at the kitchen door, and he turned with a snort of anger, staring at but not seeing a small fieldstone building not bigger than a shed at the back of the lawn, near the trees that marked the back of the estate. And when it finally came into focus, he frowned and walked over, walked around it in puzzlement because he'd never seen it before.

There was a padlock, unfastened, and with a glance at the house he removed it and opened the door. But it wasn't the dark that drove him back into the open, nor the scuffed footprints in the dust; it was the odor.

The death smell he'd encountered the night he found Peter Reskin.

The wind, sighing; the dampness turning to a light drizzle that dripped slowly off the leaves.

He pounded on the front door again, fear and anger keeping him at it until, at last, he heard the lock turning over.

The door opened, and he pushed in without waiting for an invitation.

"I want to see—"

The Long Night of the Grave

He stopped in the half-light that barely reached the ceiling of the Hall's expansive foyer, aware of the silence, the cold, the shapes and turns of darkness that filled the corners and rippled over the bare floor.

Khirhal Bey stood by the entrance to the living room, hands clasped in front of him, only his face and white shirt visible in the dusk that settled in the house.

"Where is he?" John demanded.

"Mr. Isle is not to be disturbed," the man answered stiffly.

John took a step toward him. "And you're a servant now, not a guest?"

The Egyptian did not move.

"Where *is* he?"

"Mr. Isle, as I told you—"

John waved him silent and started for the stairs at the far end of the foyer.

"Mr. Vicar."

John ignored him, grabbing the ball of the newel post to haul himself up, his hand running along the polished banister as he looked up toward the landing where the stairs split to rise right and left.

"Jeffrey!" he called. "Jeff, it's me, John!"

Darkness greeted him; no sound but the wind.

"Jeff?"

"Mr. Vicar, please."

There was a small table beside the staircase, and on it, in the dim light, he saw a tiny book, bound in dark leather, and on the cover a gold-etched figure of a jackal-headed man.

Jesus, he thought, and started to climb.

"Mr. Vicar."

At the landing he looked down. Bey had not moved, though his face was raised, his head trembling slightly as if he were a blind man seeking the source of a noise.

"Jeff!" he called again.

A footstep on the top stair, the groan of a riser.

His eyes narrowed as he tried to peer through the darkness. "Jeff?"

"Mr. Isle is rather busy," Yasfiera Bey said, stepping out of the night into twilight, her hood thrown back, her eyes painted round in blue. Red lips that glistened as if they had drunk fresh blood. "I'm sure you'll understand."

"I want to talk to him," he said, taking a step up to meet her.

"That's not possible."

He could feel it then as she stared at him without moving, a cold and empty force that made the hairs on his nape stir, made his fingers clench and open.

He backed away.

She followed, the husk of her cloak, the whisper of her gown, the silence of her soles as they took another step down.

"I need to talk to him," he said. "About the bowl."

He didn't realize he had reached the bottom until he felt Khirhal standing beside him. He whirled away, afraid of being struck though the man's hands remained clasped and his eyes remained unfocused. Yasfiera stopped at the landing, a dark shadow in darkness.

"Jeff!" he yelled. "Jeffrey, can you hear me?"

Khirhal moved then, herding him slowly toward the door.

"The bowl, Mr. Vicar," Yasfiera said, in a whisper that filled the house, and filled him with dread.

"That is something for Mr. Isle and I to discuss," he said, more bravely than he felt.

"The bowl," she repeated.

He started when the door thumped against his back, and he started again when Khirhal opened it without seeming to move. His hands felt gloved in ice. When he swallowed, he felt daggers. And when he backed onto the porch, Khirhal Bey

nodded to him once, whispered, "It's too late, my friend," and gently, very gently, closed the door in his face.

Chapter 13

W hen the storm exploded over the village an hour past noon, there had been little warning save for the gathering of the wind, a swift darkening of the sky. A brilliant flare of lightning, a concussion of thunder, and the rain slanted in glistening sheets, drumming on slate roofs and rattling across panes, quickly filling the gutters and swelling the streams. Birds were driven to their nests, horses plunged in their stalls, pedestrians on Centre Street were drenched to the skin before they could find the safety of a shop, the temporary lee of a doorway that was no refuge at all when the wind abruptly changed.

Lightning, and thunder, and the screaming crack of a bole as an elm split and fell, the prolonged groan of carved granite as a headstone toppled in the mud, the silent rending of thick velvet when a branch lunged through a window.

Vera Avlock shrieked hysterically until the servants rushed into the bedroom and quickly disposed of the limb and stuffed rags into the break. Sterling stood in the doorway, hands on his hips, demanding to know what had interrupted his nap, didn't anyone remember they had a dinner party that evening and he needed his rest?

Freddy cowered in the cluttered large closet, his eyes tightly shut, whimpering as he pulled a worn blanket to his chin, holding a stout length of wood across his quivering thighs, flinching at each thunderous peal, ducking his head when lightning ripped through the valley.

It had taken him most of Thursday to follow the secret way to his aunt's empty home, but no one had seen him and that's all that mattered. He was bad, very bad, for not going to work, but as soon as he had heard that Mr. Emmett was dead, he knew too that the graveyard was no place to be for someone like him.

For someone who had seen monsters that no one believed in.

And the moment he reached the cottage, he gathered all the food he could carry from the sparsely laden kitchen, the blankets from Gert's sagging bed, the pillows, a lantern he made sure was filled and working. Then he locked the doors front and back and crawled into the closet, jammed a length of firewood under the latch, and pushed himself into the corner.

Waiting.

Listening.

Feeling the night grow darker, grow heavier, and fill with the mist that seeped up through the floorboards.

He said his prayers a hundred times, and a hundred times again, all the while trying to remember what he had seen that horrid day. Something he only vaguely understood that Mr. Vicar should know. But his mind kept wandering, and he wept at his failure, and chewed on a knuckle to bring on the pain that would force him to think, that would force him to remember.

While the night passed, and the wind rose, and the mist touched his face.

While the storm raged and shook the house and shattered the windows, slammed open the front door.

While he cried out at the lightning, and screamed when he recognized the scent of burning wood.

———

John sat in his study and stared at the bowl, willing it to tell him what he knew was hidden there and could not see because something was standing in the way, like a shadow. Part of it, he understood, was the unreasoning fear he'd experienced the night before, the way Yasfiera Bey and her brother had looked at him, spoken to him, and finally had driven him away.

He had barely slept.

He refused to dream.

And when the Karragans didn't show up in the morning, he knew they were waiting for the storm to blow itself out.

Every lamp was lit then, every light switch thrown, and still he couldn't banish the clinging damp cold, or the shadows inside that worked to strangle his soul.

He stared, and he rummaged yet again through his books, and just shy of sunset he sat up, his finger on a page that held a picture of the darkshadow.

The house whispered to itself as the storm seemed to linger directly above, panes trembling, boards creaking, the flames in the fireplace curling away from a draught; a shutter banging, a hinge squealing, the fingernail scrape of a branch over glass.

"Impossible," he whispered. And, "Impossible!" much louder.

It was several minutes before he heard someone pounding on the front door.

He rubbed his eyes as he stood, rubbed them again and stretched as he walked slowly up the hall, glad for the interruption, relieved for the sudden breaking of the spell.

The pounding; and the storm.

"I'm coming," he muttered. "Hold on, I'm coming."

It was Jeffrey, his cloak wind-wrapped about his chest, his hair whipping at his eyes, rain running from his shoulders to puddles at his feet.

"God," John exclaimed in relief and standing aside, "am I glad to see you. I've been—"

"I can't come in," Isle told him curtly. "I have to know, John, if you're going to give me the bowl."

He squinted and turned his head away from a burst of blue-white lightning followed immediately by a peal of thunder that made his ears ring. "Jeff, this is wrong. I've already told you—"

"I know that, damn you," Isle said, nearly yelling. "And I've told you that you don't understand."

"Then for God's sake, man, take the time to explain!"

Jeffrey glared at him before whirling away and stomping off the porch, heedless of the rain, braced against the wind. In the middle of the walk, he turned and raised a fist. "You're a fool, John Vicar!" he cried over the storm. "You're a goddamned stubborn foo!!"

John strode onto the porch with every intention of grabbing the man and dragging him back into the house. But he stopped. There was a carriage waiting on the Pike, and as Isle climbed in, he could see someone else. A figure in a dark hood, who leaned over and stared at him, red lips in a smile.

He threw up a hand as if to protect himself from a blow, quickly stepped back inside and slammed and locked the door; a sudden weakening of his knees made him lean against it and marvel at the perspiration dripping from his brow.

Then he ran to the study and grabbed up the bowl, held it tightly in his left hand while he stared at the page.

Blackshadow.

A walking dead man.

Several thousand years old.

———

The crop twitched in her hand, and Betty told herself that using it on Sterling wouldn't be the worst mistake she'd ever made. Nevertheless, she did her best to hold her temper while her brother-in-law paraded across the hearth, alternately bellowing demands at the Almighty and throwing demands at her. At one point during his tirade, she feared he was going to throw a glass of brandy in her face, which made her retreat to the living room entrance, still in her riding clothes, though she'd been home for hours, arriving just barely ahead of the storm.

"Do you have any idea," he said acidly, "what sort of impression you're making around here, my dear?"

She shrugged. "Does it matter?"

"It certainly matters if my sister-in-law brings disgrace upon this good house by insisting on looking like a common slut."

The crop twitched again, and a fire burned in her cheeks. "Then would it matter," she said, snapping the words like so many whips, "if your sister-in-law ordered you out of her house?"

He laughed. "You wouldn't dare!"

"I am my father's daughter more than my sister is," she told him contemptuously. "I would dare. And unless you apologize, I shall dare."

He sneered and turned away, resting an arm along the mantel. "Rebellion doesn't suit you," he said disdainfully. "Now do as you're told, child-get out of those dreadful clothes and into something decent. Don't you realize we're having guests tonight? My god, first that damned window, and now this! Am I never going to have things go right for a change?"

She laughed; she couldn't help it. When he was posturing, she often wondered why he'd not gone on the stage.

The Long Night of the Grave

"And wash yourself," he continued, wrinkling his nose. "Good lord, you'll never marry if you insist on behaving like that."

"Like what?" she asked innocently. "A common slut? Or an uncommon one?"

"Your language, woman!" he yelled, red-faced.

"Go to hell, Sterling," she said calmly. "Save it for Vera. She thinks it's impressive."

And before the sputtering man could say another word, she stalked out of the room, lashing at the walls, the banister, as she retreated to her room. Slammed the door. Threw the crop against the vanity and only stared when several perfume vials toppled to the floor.

"God!" she shouted then. "God, I *hate* him!"

And shouted, "What!" to a timid knock on the door, groaning when Vera poked her head into the room.

"Are you all right, dear?"

She slumped onto the bed and struggled to pull off her boots. "Of course I'm not all right. That husband of yours—"

"Enough!" Vera said, striding across the carpet to stand in front of her, arms folded across her chest. "I do not want to hear another word, do you understand me, Betty? We've worked very hard for tonight, and you are not going to spoil it."

Betty tossed the boot against the wall, yanked off the other one and held it in her lap. "What do you mean?" she asked, her temper finally subsiding enough for her to hear.

"It was going to be a surprise."

"What surprise?"

Vera drew herself up. "The announcement of your engagement."

Betty felt her mouth open, felt herself leaping to her feet, and couldn't stop her hand from grabbing her sister's shoulder. "What the hell are you talking about?"

"To Jeffrey Isle, dear," Vera said, shaking off the hand as if it were little more than dust. "Sterling and I have decided you're going to marry Jeffrey Isle."

———

Sydney Edmunds stood at the window of his front room, watching the storm scream down Chancellor Avenue, watching a hackney run ahead of it toward the depot. He sighed and lit a cigar. He sighed again and let the drapery fall from his hand, wishing he could think of some way to excuse himself tonight. He was tired. He needed his sleep. He was getting too old to travel for so long at one time and then be expected to be genial at a dinner where he knew there would be bombast and petty temper displays.

He paced the room aimlessly, lifting a shoulder at a strike of lightning, closing his eyes at the thunder.

He stopped only once, to gaze into a glass-and-teak case he kept in the far corner. Lamplight glowed off the gold figure displayed there, on black velvet, and he shuddered when he imagined the jackal's head turned, and the eyes lifted to watch him.

It was then that he decided he would go.

And he would bring the damned figurine with him.

If Jeffrey wanted it so badly, then he could have it, and that was that. He doubted John would argue very strongly, and he didn't care what Turnbell thought. Reskin was dead. What was the use of being stubborn?

For the first time that day, he smiled.

But he couldn't ignore the storm that refused to let the fire warm him.

———

The Long Night of the Grave

The telephone lines were down, and Howard Turnbell swore loudly as he dropped the receiver to its cradle. All day he'd been trying to get hold of his wife, to tell her to send their regrets to the Avlocks. He had no intention of going back there this week, not if that cow, Vera, was going to flirt with him again, and not if Sterling was going to trot out his obsequious, obnoxious speeches aimed at improving his credit while, at the same time, trying to convince one and all that Betty didn't hold the purse strings, not to mention most of the family's brains.

The hell with them all, he thought as he stalked across the office; and the hell with this stupid thing, he thought as he reached into the wall safe and pulled out the scarab, wrapped in red silk. As soon as he got home, he was going to summon a messenger and send it off to John. Let him do what he wants; this piece of junk had brought him nothing but trouble.

Lightning flared, the lights flickered, and Turnbell said, "Oh hell," as he shoved the scarab into his pocket.

The echo of footsteps off stone, voices muffled behind cloth, and the wailing wind seeking a way to fall closer to the ground.

"They will be together tonight."

"I don't care. It's madness. You'll be pointing a finger straight at us."

"The storm will be our cloak. By the time it is over, my darling, it won't matter if they know it or not."

Echoes.

And footsteps.

And the keening of the wind.

"And what about him? Can we trust him?"

"We can. Until we need him no longer."

"Are you sure of that? I mean, are you really sure?"

"We have the book, my love. He has the words, but we have the book. Once it is done, we'll need him no longer."

"I can't help it. I'm worried."

A match lit and held high, flickering light off red hair and black.

"I love you," she said.

"And I you," he answered.

"Tonight," she said, brushing his lips with a kiss. "A long night, my dear Jeffrey. It belongs to the grave."

Chapter 14

Khirhal Bey thrown from the black gelding just as he reached the cemetery gates. A bolt of lightning just up the street, a charred and smoking branch sparking to the ground, and the horse reared in terror, screaming, eyes white and ears flat. He slid from the saddle before he could grab the mane, and landed in the road, rolled over and covered his head to protect himself from the hooves that lashed blindly out before taking the gelding into the early night.

He groaned softly as he sat up and wiped mud from his face, groaned loudly as he pushed himself unsteadily to his feet. A trembling hand raised as if to call the animal back, then he staggered to the gates and forced them open, slipped through, and held onto the bars until his legs stopped their quaking.

Lightning, and thunder; the headstones flared and vanished, the trees creaked in their twisting, his feet slipped several times, nearly dropping him again.

The rain paused, the wind sighed to a lull, and he broke into a hasty trot, one hand pressed against his side, his eyes narrowed in pain, his lips parted in a grotesque smile.

The mausoleum then, and around the fence to the back where he pulled at the loose bars and tossed them aside, moaning when his arm moved, nearly collapsing when bile flooded his throat and made him turn his head sharply to empty his mouth.

No sound but the dripping of water from the leaves.

No movement until he made his way across the wet grass and sagged against the marble wall, eyes closed, lungs working for a breath; turning when the pain subsided, lifting a hand head high and pressing against the corner of a stained block.

A rumbling.

The wind.

A narrow section of the wall turning inward, revealing a flight of stairs that led deep into the ground.

The rain.

He fell forward against the inner wall, slipped and slid down the steps into the chamber below where he slumped to the floor and covered his face with his hands.

Not now, he ordered to the agony inside; not now, it cannot be, there are things we must do.

Taking slow shallow breaths, then, he stripped off his wet clothes and donned the raiments of the supplicant to the master he served. Then he took the wooden bowl and placed it on the shallow iron plate over the brazier where a single breath brought him flame that he watched for a full minute. He opened the chest next and took out a handful of long narrow leaves, took the figurine's head off and brought the body to the fire.

He poured the oil.

He watched it heat.

He dropped the leaves in one by one, stepped back, and began to pray.

For an hour he said the words he had learned from the stolen book, the tablet of prayers the heathen Reskin had stolen from his people; for an hour he watched the silent fire, watched the black smoke from the boiling leaves, nearly swooned at the fragrance that began to fill the room in spite of the wind cascading down the stairs.

Then he picked up the bowl. not feeling the burning, and poured the libation drop by drop at the foot of the stone cabinet.

The Long Night of the Grave

"Sakhtu," he whispered as each drop boiled on the floor. "Sakhtu, it is time."

———

Freddy scrambled on hands and knees into the woods as the fire bellowed through the cottage. Sparks spiraled on the wind, pinpricks on the back of his neck, the backs of his hands, smoldering on the back of his long tattered coat. He didn't look around, nor did he look side to side; he kept his gaze on the trees that leaned away from him in the storm.

He remembered.

He knew what Mr. Vicar had to be told.

But Gert Naysmith's house was dying, and he couldn't stop crying, and finally he dropped to his stomach and wept against the mud, sobbing and moaning and beating the ground with his fists because it was his fault the lightning had found where he was hiding, his fault the monsters were still chasing him in his dreams.

He was frightened.

The house was burning.

And when the storm returned in a great fall of thunder, he· leapt to his feet and began running.

———

Cab Planter lay on the wooden bench in the station's front room, his hat for a pillow, his feet crossed at the ankles. He hated staying home on a miserable night like this; there was no one he could complain to, no one he could hold, and those on the night watch were better than nothing.

The telephone rang, and he stared at the empty desk, grunted to his feet and pushed through the gate. When he picked up the receiver and held it to his ear, all he could hear was a faint hissing, like someone whispering from the grave.

"Jesus," he said to Alden when the sergeant came back into the room, "this is gonna be one hell of a night."

———————

The doors of the stone cabinet opened without a sound.

Khirhal Bey bowed his head and gave the blackshadow the first of three names.

———————

"There is never," Howard Turnbell snarled to the empty office, "anyone around when you need them. Jesus, this world is going straight to hell in a handbasket and nobody gives a damn!"

He was standing in his office, coat and hat on, gloves in one hand. A messenger had come to him an hour before, requesting an urgent meeting, there in the bank. Had it been anyone else but Syd Edmunds he would have given the messenger an answer that would have curled the kid's hair; but for friendship's sake, he waited, and waited for the hour before his patience grew thin and he turned off the lights.

"The hell with him, " he muttered as he backed out of the office and locked the door behind him. "The hell with them all."

Then he dropped the key into his pocket and turned around, and for a moment his ill humor passed as he surveyed his domain—the checkered marble floor, the gleaming marble pillars, the elegant desks, the tellers' cages, the paintings on the wall and the mural on the ceiling. Lit now only by the glow of a streetlamp outside, the high and wide windows running with rain and running blacksnake shadows across the floor.

A deep breath as if he could smell and taste the money; a satisfied smile and a slow shake of his head.

He would be generous. He would stand here, in his kingdom, and give Syd another chance. But he would not speculate; speculation was for fools like Jeffrey Isle and poor young John. He would wait for five minutes before going home, to the warmth of his fire, his brandy, and the clever chatter of a wife he'd been with forty years.

He smiled.

He adjusted his hat.

He saw the large shadow pass across the window and pause at the doors.

Your five minutes are up, Syd, he thought as he pulled on his gloves.

A shadowarm lifted, and fell against the frame, an echo in the empty room, hollow and loud.

Turnbell started forward, his mood broken, his heels firm. "We're closed, you idiot," he called. "Don't you know the time?"

The shadowarm again, and the heavy frame trembled.

"Damn you," the banker muttered in disgust, quickening his pace and raising his voice. "Come back tomorrow! We're closed, damnit, we're closed!"

And the doors shattered inward, splinters cast by the wind, rain sweeping across the marble.

Turnbell cried out in anger, and cursed because he'd left his walking stick back in the office.

Then he saw it in the doorway.

"My god," he whispered. "My god, who are you?"

It stepped over the wreckage, sending its shadow out before it, pushing Turnbell back a pace until he spun around with a gasp and ran for his office. There was a special telephone line there, connecting the bank directly to the police station; he would use it, he would be all right, be wouldn't look around though he heard the footsteps following-slow, and heavy, crushing wood and glass, while the wind tilted with the paintings and cleared the desks of all their papers, and why, he thought in panic, wouldn't the goddamned key fit?

A fearful glance over his shoulder, and he snapped his head back around, to stare at the keyhole, watch his hands insert the key, watch his fingers slip off, grab hold, slip off and grab again.

The door opened.

A desk was tossed aside, crashing into the wall like the thunder detonating outside.

"No," the banker gasped as he slammed the door and locked it. "No," as he ran to the wall phone and lifted the receiver.

The door shuddered.

The wind slipped in underneath.

A crank, then two, then one again, and the door exploded, the blackshadow stepped in.

Turnbell felt his heart racing, felt his legs begin to weaken, and he almost made it to his desk and the gun in the center drawer before the blackshadow's hand closed around his neck.

He screamed.

He lashed out with his fists and his feet.

He looked into its face, and saw his kingdom explode.

———

Sgt. Alden stared sullenly at the board on the wall behind him. There were ten rows of red lights, five lights across, and the third one, third row, was blinking in time to a soft chime from a bell mounted above.

"It's the damned storm," he said, getting out of his chair to slap the board's side. "Always happens in a damned storm."

Planter, once more reclined on the bench, was tempted to agree. He had no wish to go out there tonight, no wish to get soaked to the skin just because some old maid or old man working late in a shop had panicked at a shadow.

Then he sighed and pushed himself up.

Unfortunately. this wasn't a shop. It was a bank. Worse, it was Howard Turnbell's bank, and if someone didn't go over there and have a look around, Stockton when he returned would have Planter's scalp.

"Hell," he said, and reached for his coat.

"You going?" Alden asked in surprise.

"Yep. Have to. Get your hat, you need the fresh air."

"Me?" Alden scowled. "It's raining out there!"

"Right."

"Jeez, c'mon, Cab, have a heart."

"Your coat, Tom," he said.

"But it's the storm, I tell you!"

"And if it isn't? You want to tell Turnbell?"

Alden sighed. "Damn. Planter, you know, you're a goddamned pain in the ass."

John listened to the return of the storm and decided he would pass on the dinner tonight. He needed time to think, because he'd done too much thinking already, and every answer he could find always sent him back to the page where he saw the blackshadow, lying in a sarcophagus, arms folded across its chest. And beneath the sketch the. legend that claimed the body belonged to a minor priest who called himself Sakhtu.

On the page the eyes were closed.

He shuddered and went to the phone, and cursed when he heard the dead silence of a dead line. With Karragan gone, there was no way now he'd be able to get in touch with the Avlocks. He would have to go. Indeed, perhaps it would be better that he did. Then he would be able to talk with someone about what he had found, and they in turn would tell him what an ass he was being.

Betty would laugh and show her concern, Syd would bluster and Howard would scoff, and it would be worth it even to hear Jeffrey sneer.

He started to snap off the light, then changed his mind. Instead, he scribbled a note reminding the Karragans of his invitation just in case they should return. All he needed now to complete the day would be Mary carping at him for scaring her half to death, not being home when she stepped in the door. He brought it to the hall and left it on the table, in the center of the silver plate where the calling cards should be.

Say, Betty, he thought, turning toward the stairs, did you know that there's a dead man walking around Oxrun Station? Syd, old man, I have solved another murder and you won't believe the killer's name.

"Johnny," he told himself as he hurried to his room to dress, "this is crazy. *You're crazy.*"

But on the page the eyes were closed.

Chapter 15

Freddy tumbled from the trees onto Williamston Pike, heedless of the clinging mud, the dead grass across his chest. He tripped into a run, arms spread to give him balance, mouth open to give him air. He ignored the rain lashing his face, ignored the stinging the fire had lashed to his skin. He could only see the road ahead, the way it shimmered in the lightning, the way it tilted left and right to throw him off his stride, the way it stretched into a tunnel and shrank to a serpent's back.

He ran.

And he cried.

And a branch cracked off a pine tree and cracked across his skull.

———

"Not bad," John told himself as he examined his reflection in the mirror that stood framed beside his closet. The evening jacket was cut a bit too snugly for his comfort, and the collar was impossibly stiff, but the cravat was finally right and the shirt had stopped bunching at the waist, and he liked the way the black-and-gold waistcoat gave him just that right touch of ostentation. Sterling, he thought, will have a field day with that, and he grinned and hummed all the way down to the foyer.

A hesitation; and an order not to think about a thing until he was at the house.

A loud sigh to compete weakly with the thunder, and he hurried through the first floor rooms, making sure the windows were locked, the draperies drawn, before taking up coat and hat and heading for the kitchen.

Still humming as he pulled on his gloves.

Leaving the overhead light burning so he wouldn't come home to an empty house.

Then he decided to bring the bowl with him, to show them, and explain, and force Jeff into the truth. So he took it from the study and slipped it into a deep pocket on the inside of the coat, returned to the kitchen and assured himself he was right.

Throwing open the door and swearing at the rain that drenched him within seconds.

He ran for the stable and laughed when the roan backed deeper into its stall. "A rotten night," he agreed as he calmed it with a word, stroking its muzzle, scratching it behind the ears. "But we have things to do, my friend, and this time you're not deserting me. I'll be damned if I'm going to walk home again."

The roan snorted.

He saddled it quickly before it could protest, and mounted it smoothly, led it to the door and showed it the storm.

"See?" he said, patting and rubbing its neck. "Nothing to it, pal. You just get your feet wet and everything will be fine."

The horse shied at the first strike of lightning, but John urged it outside, then prodded it into a trotting the animal soon changed to a fast canter. He didn't protest; he was just as anxious to get back under shelter as it was, and he kept his head low as they rode down the Pike, watching nothing but the road ahead until they reached the Avlock gates.

He swerved in then, and the roan galloped to the portico where a manservant was waiting to take the reins. John thanked him, the man smiled and was immediately pulled off his feet when the horse started for home. It was several minutes before the two of them were able to get the animal back under control, and several minutes more before John was convinced it would be securely stabled for the night.

Then he knocked on the door, one hand anchoring his hat, and made a great show of entering. blowing warmth on his hands and shaking the rain from his shoulders, when Betty answered.

"Only for you," he said, handing coat and hat over to a maid. "Only for you, my dear, would I be dumb enough to go out on a night like this."

But her smile was sickly, and his own smile became a frown as he took her arm above her white gloves and led her off to one side of the center hall.

"Problems?"

She shrugged. but the red on her cheeks he knew wasn't rouge.

"Sterling," he guessed.

"He wants me married."

"All right," he said, glancing into the living room where he heard low voices. "So get married."

"He wants me to marry Jeffrey."

"Jesus." He held her at a distance. "Is that what tonight's all about?"

"It wasn't supposed to be." Her eyes glittered then with unfallen tears. "The bastard. I marry Jeff. you see, and then he owns it all. Then dear Sterling buys it from him, and …"

He hushed her with a finger, offered her his arm, and they stepped into the other room, where Sterling was at his post, Vera on the couch, and Yasfiera Bey in a wing-chair, laughing quietly at a jest.

"Where are the others?" he whispered as Vera rose to greet him, her smile polite and her offered hand limp.

"You're the first," Betty whispered back.

"John," Sterling greeted expansively, stepping off the hearth to shake his hand. "Good to see you! What a horrid night, don't you think? I'm surprised you were able to make it." He looked to the front window. "I have a feeling Howard and Sydney aren't going to show. Can't blame them, though, can you? Beastly storm. Rotten. Care for a brandy?"

John watched him perform his hostly duties, suspicion strong in his expression, which Avlock studiously ignored. Then he took a seat on the couch facing Vera's, and Betty sat beside him.

"So, John," Sterling said, "I suppose my lovely sister-in-law has told you the good news?"

———

Khirhal Bey tipped the bowl again.

And whispered the second name.

———

Sydney cursed the perverse behavior of his tie, finally yanked it off his neck and threw it on the floor. He had half a mind to change his plans and not go. It was bad enough his waist fought him every step of the way as he struggled to put on his trousers and shoes; now his fat fingers were betraying him as well, making him out the fool, making him helpless.

He grunted.

He retrieved the tie and within seconds had it perfect.

"You shouldn't think, " he told himself as he picked up a hair brush. "The thing is, Syd, you can't think about it, or it'll muck up."

A touch of powder to his neck; a touch of scent to his jaw. A whisk that took the lint from his lapels and brocade waistcoat, a check of the gold pocket watch to be sure it was right.

Thunder that shook the house.

He grinned at the lamps burning on every table, thinking of the poor fools who had electricity, and were most likely ready to sue everyone in sight because the storm had probably knocked out the power. That sort of aggravation was not for him. Bad enough the railroads were being struck left and right, and his investments threatened the longer the strikes lasted; he wasn't going to complicate matters by bringing in something he couldn't control.

He stepped back from the mirror and turned around, looked over his shoulder and tugged at the jacket's hem.

"Not bad for lard," he said with a rueful laugh, and picked up a silver-headed cane from the bed and hurried downstairs, where he made sure the fire was still burning properly in its place, the lamps were still filled and lit, the back and veranda doors locked and barred. Then he decided he would warm himself with a small brandy.

He had time.

The carriage wasn't scheduled to arrive for another fifteen minutes.

He had time.

Too much time, he thought then, as he took the first sip and shuddered at the burning that made him cough into a fist. It was on nights like this when he wished he had a wife. Someone who would fuss over him, to admire him ... to convince him to stay home where he would have a better time than with that stuffy Sterling Avlock. There had been mistresses, on occasion, and once there'd been an engagement. But that had been when he was younger, and not ready to settle down.

Another sip, and he sniffed, put down the glass and walked over to the corner.

In the display case the jackal-headed man stared blindly at his stomach, and he opened the top. lifted it out, and held it across both hands.

Beautiful, he thought, bringing it closer to his eyes; age does you well, my friend, and a hell of a lot better than it treats me, don't you think?

There was a loud knock on the door.

He looked at the clock on the mantel.

A second knock, more like a pounding, and he set the figurine back before crossing the room to the foyer.

"All right," he called. "All right, I'm coming. Hold your horses."

Grabbing up his hat and raincloak, he reached for the knob just as the door's central panel splintered inward, driving him back with a shout.

A hand, an arm, swathed in grey cloth darkened by the rain, filling the house with a stench that made him gag as he stumbled away into the front room; a hand that gripped the wood and pulled it apart like paper, pulled the door off its hinge and threw it into the night.

Edmunds held the cane protectively across his chest while he fumbled for the telephone on the wall near the hearth. "I have a gun!" he shouted as the wind tore at the draperies, the rain covered the foyer rug. "I'll shoot, I swear I will!"

He lifted the receiver and waited for the operator's voice, muttering, "Come on, you old cow, where the hell are you?"

Then it stepped into the room, and the receiver fell from his hands.

"Jesus God," he said, and threw the cane as hard as he could at the blackshadow coming toward him, pushing aside the couch, toppling a table whose lamp shattered on the floor and spilled flaming oil on the carpet.

The Long Night of the Grave

"Jesus God," he said again, and ran for the dining room. But his left foot caught the display case's leg, and he stumbled sideways, turning, the case falling, the glass breaking, the figurine rolling across the floor into the fast-spreading flames.

The blackshadow reached down as Edmunds watched, and he could have sworn that it groaned as it picked up the statuette and held it over its head.

The couch began to burn, the draperies, the walls.

Edmunds shook his head in denial and opened his mouth to scream, but the jackal-headed man spun through the air and caught him on the temple. He moaned as he fell, blood blinding his right eye and running down his jowls; he moaned again when he hit the floor and rolled onto his back, eyes wide in disbelief as the blackshadow stood over him, its outline shimmering in the rising heat, the writhing light behind.

John, he thought, and thought nothing but a scream when the hand took his throat and lifted him to his feet, lifted him off the floor and held him high.

Weightless.

Legs thrashing.

Until it turned and dropped the fat man into the mouth of the fire.

Cab Planter stood in the middle of Turnbell's office, smoking a cigarette he couldn't taste, waiting for Dr. Gravell to get to the bank. He had already sent a loudly protesting Alden on to fetch John Vicar, and now he was sorry he hadn't gone with him.

He didn't like being here, not alone, not with the lightning playing tricks with the shadows, not with the battered body of the old man still bleeding across the desk; and not being able to turn away from what the old man held in his hand.

Impossible, he thought, and was relieved when the doctor came, took one look at Turnbell, and said, "You'd better get John, Cab. This is something he ought to see."

I'm dead, Freddy thought; *I'm dead, I'm dead*. The rain fell into his open mouth, and he choked and rolled over.

I'm dead. I'm dead.

Thunder stoppered his ears.

Wind-driven mud slapped against his cheek until he rolled onto his back again, and sat up, grinning.

Not dead, he told himself, and cried out at the pain that stretched across his scalp. There was too much rain to tell if he was bleeding, but he remembered with the next peal where he was going, what he was going to say. And he jumped up, swayed, and broke into a shambling run, telling himself the pain was good because he wasn't dead, he was alive, and Mr. Vicar would save him from the monsters in the storm.

Running from one verge to the other, calling Vicar's name, falling against the wall that fronted Vicar's house. He grinned. He fell through the gate. He fell against the door and pounded on it with both fists.

No one answered.

"Mr. Vicar!"

No one came to the door.

"Mr. Vicar!"

His head hurt, there were pictures of dark things in there, and he grabbed the knob and turned it, and stood dumbly when the door opened.

Wrong, Freddy, he thought as he stepped over the threshold; this is bad, you'll get in trouble, you're going to get in real bad trouble if you don't get out now.

The Long Night of the Grave

Then lightning flared and pushed his shadow toward the back, and he jumped farther in, one hand to his mouth, blinking away the rain that dripped from his hair. Finally staring at the paper the wind shoved to the floor.

Chapter 16

John smiled stiffly as Avlock prattled on about how wonderful the night was in spite of the storm, feeling Betty stiffen at his side whenever Jeffrey's name was mentioned. Yasfiera, however, remained curiously silent, and several times he caught her glancing nervously toward the door.

"I wouldn't worry about Jeff," he said at last, his tone forcing the woman to look at him, eyes wide. "I have what he wants. In fact, I've brought it with me. He'll be here sooner or later."

"I do not understand," she said in a low voice.

"Neither do I, exactly," he answered. "But I will. I assure you, I will."

Avlock cleared his throat then, loudly enough to turn John's attention. "As I was saying—"

Yasfiera stood then, reaching behind her to grip the back of her chair. "Excuse me," she said faintly. "I should like to …"

Immediately, Vera rose. "Oh, my dear, of course." She took Yasfiera's arm and led her to the stairs. "I can't imagine what's keeping the others. I'm sure Jeffrey will be here before long. It's this storm, you know. It's practically ruined everything."

They listened to her babbling until it was too faint to hear, then Sterling sniffed and took a long pull at his drink. "A strange woman," he said, nodding toward the stairs. "Foreign, if you know what I mean."

"More foreign than you or I know," John said, aware of the look Betty suddenly gave him.

"Damn right," Avlock said. And said, "Damn," again when someone began banging frantically on the door. He stomped across the room and vanished into the foyer, then yelled so loudly John scrambled to his feet and followed.

"Freddy!" he exclaimed, when he saw Jones struggling with Avlock to gain entrance to the house.

"Mr. Vicar!" the disheveled man cried. "Mr. Vicar, the leaves! The leaves! I remember the leaves!"

Avlock slapped the man in the chest. knocking him onto his back on the porch, and John ran forward, shoving Sterling aside and dropping to his knees. There was blood on Jones' face, his clothes were torn and burned, and he snapped an order over his shoulder for someone to help carry him into the house.

"The hell," Avlock said, but was prevented from slamming the door when Betty elbowed past him, took one look at Freddy, and called back into the house for the servants to come running.

Though Avlock protested harshly, Jones was carefully laid on one of the kitchen islands, still babbling about leaves, and groaning whenever someone tried to examine his wound. Finally, Betty gave him a glass of bourbon, most of which he dribbled down his chin; but it served to calm him, stop his weeping, and John listened to his story.

"The leaves," Freddy said. "Mr. Vicar, I forgot to tell you about the leaves in the stone house."

"What stone house, Freddy?" he asked gently.

"His," Jones answered, and pointed at Sterling.

———

Ten minutes later, John strode into the living room and stood in front of the fire. The wind howled across the chimney mouth, drew the flames upward, made them dance, but no matter how close he held his hands to the fire, he couldn't get them warm.

"John?"

A hand light on his shoulder, and he covered it with his own.

"John, what's going on?"

But his explanation was interrupted when Jeffrey stormed in without knocking, hatless, face and coat dripping. He took one look at them standing before the fireplace and demanded to know where Yasfiera was.

"Upstairs," Betty told him.

Isle took a step toward the staircase, and stopped when John said his name. "What is it?" he said angrily.

"The bowl."

"It's too late, John. I told you that before."

"I have it with me. It appears that it has upset your lady friend."

Isle entered the room without removing his coat, eyes in a wary squint. "I don't think I understand."

"Sakhtu," he said then, and silently sighed when Isle's face paled. "Oh, Jesus, Jeff, what have you gotten yourself into?"

"Nothing," said Yasfiera Bey as she took the last step· into the foyer and came up behind Jeffrey. "Nothing he does not understand. which is more than I can say for you, Mr. Vicar."

John passed a hand over his face, bowed his head for a moment. "Ceremonies," he said quietly, feeling Betty stir at his side. "I don't know what kind, and I don't exactly know what they involve, but there are ceremonies, aren't there? And for some reason they require this bowl, and the statuette, and Thornbell's scarab. It's not gambling, is it, Jeff. You lied about that." He stepped off the hearth. "I saw it, you know. I saw that *thing* the other night." Another step, and Isle seemed to hide

behind the woman without moving. "I know it killed Reskin, and Freddy's aunt, and Jake Emmett."

Isle tried and failed to sneer. "I haven't the slightest idea what you're talking about."

"Really?"

He pushed between them and went to his coat, took out the bowl, and returned to the fireplace without showing them what he carried. When he did, it was while he held it close to the flames.

"How much is it worth to you, Jeff, to stop me from dropping it?"

"My god, you don't know what you're doing!" Isle shouted, and started for him, stopping only when Yasfiera came after him and grabbed his arm.

"Don't," she said. "He will not do it."

But her voice trembled, and she would not meet his gaze.

"It's that so-called curse of yours," John said then. "Something you saw on your last trip abroad convinced you that all this hocus-pocus was going to prolong your life. Something—"

And he stopped when he saw the expression on the man's face; it was fear, and it was hatred, and it was a cold and dark contempt that almost made him consign the bowl to the flames without another word.

Betty took his arm and hugged it.

They could hear Sterling in the kitchen, arguing with the servants taking care of Freddy.

"You've done it, haven't you?" he said then, feeling pieces fall together, feeling horror cover them all. "You've brought that renegade priest's body into the country, and you've brought it back to life." He closed his eyes at the thought, at the impossibility, and opened them again when he saw the blackshadow on the road. "My god, you really have done it."

Isle reached into his coat then, and Betty gasped when he pulled out a gun, at the same time slipping his other arm around Yasfiera's waist as she placed a hand on his chest.

"To live forever, John," he said proudly. "To know the secrets, and to know the words, is to live forever." He hugged the woman more tightly. "We, John, shall do it. And you are not going to stop us."

"I'll burn it," John said, his throat suddenly dry.

Isle smiled and shook his head. "I'll kill you where you stand, old friend, and still get what I need. Why don't you hand it over now, and save your life. No. Save Mistress Betty's." And he swung the barrel of the gun toward her, his finger visibly tightening on the trigger.

John damned him with a look, and though Betty's grip told him not to do it, he drew his hand away from the fire and stared at the bowl. "All those people," he said. "They're dead because of you."

"It can't be helped. It's the way of it sometimes."

Yasfiera smiled then, and he wanted nothing more at that moment than to see her in her grave.

"The bowl, John."

Then Sterling stomped into the room, demanding at the top of his voice that someone get the half-wit out of his kitchen. Isle whirled toward him, and John instantly leapt from the hearth and slapped the bowl against his arm, sending the gun across the floor to stop at Avlock's feet. At the same time, he slammed a fist into Isle's stomach, doubling him over, a kick sending him writhing to the floor. Then he ran from the house and raced straight for the stables.

There were footsteps behind him.

He didn't look back, nor did he take the time to saddle the roan; he only touched its side, said a word, and scrambled onto its back, nearly knocking Betty over as he hurried the animal from its stall.

"John, where are you going?" she called over the wind.

"The graveyard," he shouted as the roan skittered sideways. "Stay here. I'll be back."

And he was gone, low on the animal's neck as Isle ran from the house, waving the gun uselessly in the blinding, stinging rain.

Into the dark, into the storm.

Using the roan's mane to halt it when he saw Sgt. Alden in the police carriage careening toward him.

Leaning over and glaring when he heard about Thornbell, and the fire at Sydney Edmunds'; shouting over the wind that the man should fetch Planter and meet him, with guns, at Memorial Park.

He didn't wait for an answer, but kicked the horse's ribs and bent low again when it leapt forward with a toss of its head, a baring of its teeth.

To the gates he forced open.

Along the path toward the back.

Lightning over his shoulder; thunder clapping over the graves.

Until he reached the mausoleum and saw the gap in the fence and the open passage in the wall.

———

He gave himself no time to think.

Slapping the roan's hindquarters to send it on its way, he slipped quickly through the fence and stood with his back against the wall, trying to take a breath, wiping the rain from his eyes, finally leaning over and peering down the stone staircase.

The leaves, he thought; Freddy had seen leaves and had known someone had been in the mausoleum when no one should have been here.

The bowl was in his pocket.

He touched it, swallowed, and took the first step down.

And the rain abruptly stopped. Thunder rumbling in the distance; a faint flicker of lightning. The wind settling, and the air touched with a mist that rose and turned to fog.

An inconstant light below; the scent of something strong that made him cover his mouth until he no longer felt like gagging.

And a voice—insistent and soft, chanting words he didn't know.

Downward, one step at a time.

And at the bottom, the stone room, and Khirhal Bey in blinding white kneeling on the floor, arms wide, fingers spread, facing an open cabinet in which he saw the shadow of a sarcophagus whose lid was tipped to one side. Sparks of gold, flares of diamonds.

He saw the table, the brazier, the open chest, and the dark pool of blood that gathered at the man's knees.

Suddenly Khirhal Bey realized he was not alone. He looked sharply upward and saw John in the doorway. His eyes narrowed, and relaxed, and a feral smile touched his lips.

"You are foolish, Mr. Vicar," he said without rising to his feet. "You will die when Lord Sakhtu follows you to me."

"Follows?" And he waved his hand when he understood. The blackshadow, the creature, had killed the others for the artifacts, somehow knowing where they were, and knowing now where he was.

He couldn't resist a glance behind him, and when he looked back, the Egyptian was trying to stand. But there was too much blood, too much pain, and he soon gave up the effort.

"You will die as well," he said quietly, stepping deeper into the chamber.

"It does not matter. I will live again."

John shook his head. "Not if you're hoping for help from Jeffrey Isle. The man has plans of his own, and I doubt they include you."

Khirhal Bey smiled without mirth, managed a quick mirthless laugh that soon turned to a hoarse gagging. He swayed, nearly toppled, then abruptly became rigid.

"My Lord," he whispered.

And John saw the shadow burying his own on the floor.

Chapter 17

John didn't look around until he'd put the brazier between himself and the blackshadow slowly moving down the stairs. Khirhal Bey was groaning now, whatever words or prayers there were trapped in the agony of a fresh flow of blood.

John paid him no attention; he could only stare through numbing fear at the creature moving into the light, its right arm extended while its left hand carried the statuette and the scarab. There were bloodstains on its chest, droplets shining about its shoulders, and the first blur of fog began to twist around its feet.

And the eyes where the deathwrap had been cut away on its face-nothing more than holes that revealed the same cold black emptiness of a starless winter sky. Watching him as it stood uncertain, its head slightly cocked to listen to Bey's moaning.

Then a hand grabbed at John's leg, and he lashed out to drive the dying Egyptian to his side, turning as the creature threw its burden on the floor and came at him, head palsied, legs stiff, hands out and clawed as it reached for his throat.

The fog thickened.

There were voices outside.

"Here!" John cried. "Here, I'm in here!"

Feinting a run for the stairs, and when the creature awkwardly turned, grabbing the brazier by its center and lifting it, tipping it so that the bowl on the iron plate fell off and rolled empty to the wall.

The Long Night of the Grave

The creature's bound jaw worked as if it were trying to speak; its hands still reaching, the embers glowing into low flame.

Footsteps then, and a woman's insistent voice.

It turned just as Isle and Yasfiera Bey charged into the chamber, grabbing each other when they saw Khirhal on the floor and the blackshadow watching them, indecisive in spite of the words the woman gave it in a tongue John didn't understand.

"Put it down, John," Isle said quietly, taking his hand from his pocket and showing the gun.

Yasfiera spoke again.

Blackshadow, waiting.

And John thrust the brazier out as hard as he could, the flaming coals and ash showering over the creature, its wrappings immediately bursting into flame.

Yasfiera screamed and covered her face with her hands.

Isle hesitated before firing twice, but John had already turned and threw the iron stand at him. The shots ricocheted off the ceiling; Isle crumpled to the floor, grasping the brazier where one of its raised spikes had pierced his chest, blood seeping from the corner of his mouth, his eyes opened and dazed.

Yasfiera, screaming, her flesh flaking to dust.

The blackshadow, ablaze and stumbling around the room, toppling the table, passing over Khirhal Bey and setting his robes afire.

John backed away from it all, swallowing to keep himself from joining the woman, his hands stretched behind him, searching for the entrance because he dared not take his gaze from the torch that finally found him.

Jeffrey, moaning.

Yasfiera, slowly dropping to her knees, dust and yellowed bone.

And he reached the stairs a step ahead of the creature, stumbled as he ran up, splitting the skin on one knee. Biting back a groan and running again. Falling over the top step and tumbling onto the grass where Betty and Cab Planter were racing toward him, through the fog.

He looked behind him and down, and saw the torch following still, blackshadow still clear in the colorless fire.

"John, for god's sake," Planter said, hauling him to his feet.

But John shook him off and fell against the wall, slapping at it, shouting for the others to help him, feeling his frustration growing, feeling the heat, the cold, until something gave beneath the marble and the door began to close.

"Jesus Christ," Planter whispered.

Blackshadow, and fire, and as the door sealed itself without making a sound, a sudden bellow of anguish that echoed over the graves.

————

He sat before the fire, a lap robe over his knees.

Betty knelt beside him, holding a glass of red wine.

"John," she said, as she'd said a hundred times over the past several weeks. "John."

And he stirred.

First a quivering of a hand, then a blink of an eye, and finally a wan pull at his lips to make himself smile.

"I've been away," he whispered hoarsely.

She smiled, and rose, and gave him a long gentle kiss. "You have indeed, John Vicar."

A long breath, a longer sigh.

"Poor Jeffrey," he said. "Oh my god, poor old Jeff."

Betty pulled a chair beside his, reached over and took his hand. "Sterling had another wall built over … that one. He complains that it ruins the symmetry of the thing, but he did it."

He turned his head. "You had nothing to do with it, I suppose?"

"Not I," she said, a hand to her throat. "Whatever makes you think that, John?"

The smile to a grin, and he squeezed her hand. "I'm sorry."

"For what?"

"For …" And he nodded to indicate his helplessness, the fog-filled shell he had crawled into after the marble door sealed the tomb.

"Vera says I shall have to marry you now. It just isn't proper for me to be here all the time, looking after a single man with no chaperon to be sure you won't do something dreadful."

A footstep behind the chair, and Mrs. Karragan placed a tray of drink and sandwiches on a low table. When she saw John's face, she smiled and nodded and said not a word as she hurried from the room.

"Help me up," he said then, and brooked no arguments as he pushed himself to his feet. His legs were a bit wobbly, but the shell was broken, the fog gone. and when she helped him to the porch and he saw the blue sky, felt the summer warmth, he nearly burst into tears, with both joy and sorrow.

Leo was busily trimming the shrubs by the wall.

A crow stalked the lawn, warily followed by a sparrow.

"Ned is back," Betty said as they walked toward the road.

"Oh?"

"Cab hasn't said a thing. There's some story or other, but he hasn't said a thing."

"Two bowls," he said then.

"John, please."

"No, it's all right." He took her arm, kissed her cheek. "The first set—bowl, scarab, statuette—were to bring that monster back to life when none of us would sell. The second set was for Jeffrey and Yasfiera; that was the way of it, I think, the way to keep them from dying." He shook his head. "All gone now, and somehow, it's a shame, don't you think? All that knowledge lost. Thousands of years before this country was even dreamt of, and now it's all lost."

"Past," she told him softly. "It's past, John."

"Yes," he said. "It is."

And they stood at the wall watching the trees dance, watching a flock of geese swing over the village.

"You know," he said suddenly, "I'm awfully hungry."

She laughed. "Well, you should be, you dope. You've scarcely eaten for a month."

"Then it's settled. We will have lunch before we go into town."

"John, you're not well enough yet."

"I certainly am. And if you don't want to make your sister out a liar, you'd better listen to me, woman. There are judges to see, and all those damned papers."

Betty stood away from him, her hands on her hips. "That's it?" she said. "That's all the proposal I get?"

He shrugged. "But I'm ill," he told her. "You just said so yourself. Surely you don't want me getting down on one knee and catching a chill which will give me a cold which will—"

"All right," she said. "God, you're going to be a chore, John Vicar. You're going to be one damned big chore."

He laughed and moved to embrace her, then widened his eyes when he saw a familiar figure riding down the Pike on a gleaming new bicycle. "Well, I'll be damned," he said.

Betty took his hand and they hurried through the gate. "I didn't think you'd mind," she said as Freddy Jones pedaled toward them. "Someone had to take care of the Hall until the estate was settled. And Freddy absolutely refused to set foot in the Park."

Freddy stopped in front of them, grinning broadly as he pumped John's hand until John thought his shoulder would come off.

"You look good, Freddy," he said.

"I am, Mr. Vicar," Jones said, nodding. "I'm very good. You know, Miss Jerrard, she's even teaching me to read and do my numbers."

"Is that so?"

"And he's a marvelous student," Betty said with some pride. "Nobody makes fun of him anymore, isn't that right?"

"Right," the man said, reaching into his shirt. "I can read, and I can add, and pretty soon I'm going to have my own business and be rich, just like you."

The laughter was friendly, and only John noticed what the man held in his hand.

"Every night," Freddy said. "I read every night. Out loud to myself so I can hear my mistakes."

It was a book.

"I just wish," Freddy said, "there weren't so many noises at night. They're scary, you know?"

Bound in dark leather.

"It's only the house, Freddy," Betty said.

"I guess," he said.

On the cover the figure of a jackal-headed man.

"But sometimes I think I can hear people walking."

About the Author

Photo by Jeff Schalles

Charles L. Grant taught English and history at the high school level before becoming a full-time writer in the '70s. He served for many years as an officer in the Horror Writers Association and in Science Fiction Writers of America.

He was known for his "quiet horror" and for editing the award-winning Shadows anthologies. He received the British Fantasy Society's Special Award in 1987 for life achievement; in 2000, he was the recipient of the Lifetime Achievement Award from HWA. Other awards include two Nebula Awards and three World Fantasy Awards for writing and editing.

Charlie died from a lengthy illness on September 15, 2006, just three days after his birthday. He lived in Newton, NJ, and was married to writer/editor Kathryn Ptacek for nearly twenty-five years.

Book List

Horror
Novels
Black Oak: Genesis
Black Oak: The Hush of Dark Wings
Black Oak: Winter Knight
Black Oak: Hunting Ground
Black Oak: When the Cold Wind Blows
Fire Mask
For Fear of the Night
In A Dark Dream
Jackals
Millennium Quartet #1: Symphony
Millennium Quartet #2: In the Mood
Millennium Quartet #3: Chariot
Millennium Quartet #4: Riders in the Sky
Night Songs
Raven
Something Stirs
Stunts
The Bloodwind
The Curse
The Grave
The Hour of the Oxrun Dead
The Last Call of Mourning
The Nestling
The Pet
The Sound Of Midnight
The Tea Party

The Universe of Horror Trilogy
The Soft Whisper of the Dead
The Dark Cry of the Moon
The Long Night of the Grave

Collections
Dialing the Wind
Nightmare Seasons
The Black Carousel
The Orchard

Science Fiction
A Quiet Night of Fear
Ascension
Legion
Ravens of the Moon
The Shadow of Alpha

As "Geoffrey Marsh"
The Fangs of the Hooded Demon
The King of Satan's Eyes
The Patch of the Odin Soldier
The Tail of the Arabian, Knight

As "Lionel Fenn"
The Quest for the White Duck Trilogy
Blood River Down
Web of Defeat
Agnes Day

The Kent Montana Series
The Really Ugly Thing From Mars
The Reasonably Invisible Man
The Once and Future Thing
The Mark of the Moderately Vicious Vampire

668, the Neighbor of the Beast

The Diego Series
Once Upon a Time in the East
By The Time I Get To Nashville
Time, the Semi-Final Frontier

The Seven Spears of the W'dch'ck

As "Simon Lake"
The Midnight Place Series
Daughter of Darkness
Death Cycle
He Told Me To
Something's Watching

As "Felicia Andrews"
Moonwitch
Mountainwitch
Riverrun
Riverwitch
Seacliffe
Silver Huntress
The Velvet Hart

As "Deborah Lewis"
Eve of the Hound
Kirkwood Fires
The Wind at Winter's End
Voices Out of Time

Curious about other Crossroad Press books? Stop by our
website: http://crossroadpress.com
We offer quality writing
in digital, audio, and print formats.

Subscribe to our newsletter on the website homepage and
receive a free eBook.

www.ingramcontent.com/pod-product-compliance
Lightning Source LLC
Chambersburg PA
CBHW022023170626